'Whoops!' A cool voice cut into his angry tirade and Niccolò turned to see Alannah Collins strolling into the room without bothering to knock. Suddenly his words were forgotten.

If somebody had asked him his name right then he thought he might have had trouble remembering it. And yet for a moment he almost didn't recognise her—because in his memory she was wearing very little, and the woman in front of him had barely an inch of flesh on show. It was the sound of her naturally sultry voice which had kick-started his memory and his libido. But it didn't take long for his eyes to reacquaint themselves with her magnificent body—nor to acknowledge the natural sensuality which seemed to shimmer from it in almost tangible waves.

Niccolò swallowed. He had forgotten the pale creaminess of her complexion and the rosiness of her lips. As she moved he could see the glitter of a little blue dragonfly brooch gleaming on her shirt-collar. It matched the amazing colour of her eyes. And even though he despised her he could do nothing about the leap of desire which made his body grow tense. She made him think of things he'd rather not think about—but mostly she made him think about sex.

Sharon Kendrick started story-telling at the age of eleven, and has never really stopped. She likes to write fast-paced, feel-good romances with heroes who are so sexy they'll make your toes curl!

Born in west London, she now lives in the beautiful city of Winchester—where she can see the cathedral from her window (but only if she stands on tiptoe). She has two children, Celia and Patrick, and her passions include music, books, cooking and eating—and drifting off into wonderful daydreams while she works out new plots!

Recent titles by the same author:

THE HOUSEKEEPER'S AWAKENING *(At His Service)*
SEDUCED BY THE SULTAN *(Desert Men of Qurhah)*
SHAMED IN THE SANDS *(Desert Men of Qurhah)*
DEFIANT IN THE DESERT *(Desert Men of Qurhah)*

CHRISTMAS IN DA CONTI'S BED

BY
SHARON KENDRICK

First published in Great Britain 2014
by Mills & Boon, an imprint of Harlequin (UK) Limited,
Eton House, 18-24 Paradise Road, Richmond, Surrey, TW9 1SR

© 2014 Sharon Kendrick

ISBN: 978-0-263-24341-3

Harlequin (UK) Limited's policy is to use papers that are natural,
renewable and recyclable products and made from wood grown in
sustainable forests. The logging and manufacturing processes conform
to the legal environmental regulations of the country of origin.

Printed and bound in Great Britain
by CPI Antony Rowe, Chippenham, Wiltshire

CHRISTMAS IN DA CONTI'S BED

This book lovingly acknowledges the feisty
and wonderful McCormick women—
and most especially Joan and Eileen.

CHAPTER ONE

NICCOLÒ DA CONTI hated marriage, Christmas and love—but most of all he hated it when people didn't do what he wanted them to.

An unfamiliar feeling of frustration made him bite back a graphic expletive as he paced the floor of the vast New York hotel suite. Outside, skyscrapers and stars glittered against the deepening indigo sky, though not nearly as brightly as the Christmas lights which were already adorning the city.

But Niccolò was oblivious to the party atmosphere, or even to the onset of this most hated time of year. All he could think about was his only sister and wondering why she was being so damned *disobedient*.

'I do not want,' he said, sucking in a ragged breath in an attempt to control his rapidly spiralling temper, 'some tacky topless model acting as your bridesmaid. I have worked long and hard to establish a degree of respectability in your life, Michela. Do you understand what I'm saying? It cannot be allowed to happen, and what is more—I will not allow it to happen.'

From the other side of the glitzy New York hotel penthouse suite, Michela's expression remained unchanged as she looked at him.

'But you can't stop me from having her, Niccolò,' she said stubbornly. 'I'm the bride and it's my decision. That's the thing.'

'You think so?' His mouth hardened and he felt another hot flicker of rage. 'I could refuse to pay for this wedding for a start.'

'But the man I'm marrying is rich enough to carry the cost of the marriage if you decide to take such drastic action.' Michela hesitated. 'Though I'm sure you wouldn't want the world to know that Niccolò da Conti had refused to finance his only sister's wedding, just because he doesn't approve of her choice of bridesmaid. Wouldn't that be a step too far in the modern world—even for a man as old-fashioned as you?'

Niccolò flexed and then relaxed his fingers, wishing there were a nearby punch-bag on which he could vent his mounting frustrations. The world usually ran according to his wishes and he was not used to having them questioned. Bad enough that Alekto Sarantos was acting like some kind of prima donna...without having to cope with the bombshell that Alannah Collins was here.

His mouth tightened with anger as he thought about his sister and the sacrifices he had made. For too long he had fought to keep their tiny family unit intact and he was not prepared to relinquish control over her just yet. Because old habits died hard. He had faced shame and tragedy and had seen them off. He had protected Michela as much as was within his power to do so, and now she was about to enter into marriage, which would see her secure for life. His careful vetting of would-be suitors had paid dividends and she was about to marry into one of the most powerful Italian-American families in New York. She would have the sanctity he had always wished for her and nothing would be allowed to tarnish the occasion. Nothing and no one.

Especially not Alannah Collins.

Even the *thought* of the minxy little tramp made his body react in a complicated way he found difficult to control—and he was a man who prided himself on control. A powerful combination of lust and regret flooded over him, although his overriding emotion was one of rage, and that was the one he hung onto.

'I cannot believe that she has had the nerve to show her face,' he bit out. 'I can't believe she's even here.'

'Well, she is. I invited her.'

'I thought you hadn't seen her since I withdrew you from that appalling school.'

Michela hesitated. 'Actually, we've…well, we've stayed in touch over the years,' she said. 'We emailed and phoned—and I used to see her whenever I was in England. And last year she came to New York and we took a trip to the Keys and it was just like old times. She was my best friend at school, Niccolò. We go back a long way.'

'And yet you told me nothing of this before?' he demanded. 'You maintain a secret friendship and then spring it on me on the eve of your marriage? Didn't you stop to consider how it might look—to have someone as notorious as this tawdry exhibitionist playing a major role in your wedding?'

Michela lifted her hands up to the sides of her head

in a gesture of frustration. 'Are you surprised I didn't tell you, when this is the kind of reaction I get?'

'What does Lucas say about your connection with her?' he demanded.

'It happened a long time ago. It's history, Niccolò. Most people in the States haven't even heard of *Stacked* magazine—it folded ages ago. And yes, I know that a video of the original shoot seems to have found its way onto YouTube—'

'What?' he exploded.

'But it's really quite tame by modern standards,' said Michela quickly. 'If you compare it to some of the music videos you see these days—well, it's almost suitable for the kindergarten! And Alannah doesn't do that kind of stuff any more. You've got her all wrong, Niccolò, she's—'

'She is a tramp!' he gritted out, his Sicilian accent becoming more pronounced as his temper rose once again. 'A precocious little tramp, who shouldn't be allowed within ten feet of decent society. When will you get it into your head, Michela, that Alannah Collins is—'

'Whoops!' A cool voice cut into his angry tirade and Niccolò turned to see a woman strolling into the room without bothering to knock and suddenly his words were forgotten. If somebody had asked him his name right then, he thought he might have trouble remembering it. And yet for a moment he almost didn't recognise her—because in his memory she was wearing very little and the woman in front of him had barely an inch of flesh on show. It was the sound of her naturally sultry voice which kick-started his memory and his libido. But it didn't take long for his eyes to reacquaint themselves with her magnificent body—nor to acknowledge the natural sensuality which seemed to shimmer from it in almost tangible waves.

She was wearing jeans and a white shirt with a high collar, but the concealing nature of her outfit did nothing to disguise the luscious curves beneath. Thick black hair like lustrous jet hung over her shoulders, and eyes the colour of denim were studying him with a hint of mockery in their depths. Niccolò swallowed. He had forgotten the pale creaminess of her complexion and the rosiness of her lips. He had forgotten that this half-Irish temptress with an unknown father could burrow underneath his skin, without even trying.

As she moved he could see the glitter of a little blue dragonfly brooch gleaming on her shirt-collar, which matched the amazing colour of her eyes. And even though he despised her, he could do nothing about the leap of desire which made his body grow tense. She made him think of things he'd rather not think about—but mostly she made him think about sex.

'Did I just hear my name being taken in vain?' she questioned lightly. 'Would you like me to walk back out and come in again?'

'Feel free to walk out any time you like,' he answered coldly. 'But why don't you do us all a favour, and skip the second part of the suggestion?'

She tilted her chin in a way which made her black hair ripple down her back, like an ebony waterfall. But the smile she slanted at him didn't quite reach her eyes.

'I see you've lost none of your natural charm,

Niccolò,' she observed acidly. 'I'd forgotten how you could take the word "insult" and give it a whole new meaning.'

Niccolò felt a pulse begin to pound in his temple as his blood grew heated. But much worse was the jerk of lust which made his groin feel unbearably hard. Which made him want to crush his mouth down over her lips and kiss all those insolent words away and then to drive deep inside her until she screamed out his name, over and over again.

Damn her, he thought viciously. Damn her, with all her easy confidence and her louche morals. And damn those sinful curves, which would compel a grown man to crawl over broken glass just to have the chance of touching them.

'Forgive me,' he drawled, 'but for a moment I didn't recognise you with your clothes on.'

He saw the brief discomfiture which crossed her face and something primitive gave him a heady rush of pleasure to think that he might have touched a nerve and hurt her. Hurt her as she had once hurt his family and threatened to ruin their name.

But she turned the look into a bright and meaningless smile. 'I'm not going to rise to that,' she said as she turned instead to his sister. 'Are you ready for your fitting, Michela?'

Michela nodded, but her eyes were still fixed nervously on Niccolò. 'I wish you two could be civil to each other—at least until the wedding is over. Couldn't you do that for me—just this once? Then you never need see one another again!'

Niccolò met Alannah's speculative gaze and the thought of her smiling serenely in a bridesmaid gown made his blood boil. Didn't she recognise that it was hypocritical for her to play the wide-eyed innocent on an important occasion such as this? Couldn't she see that it would suit everyone's agenda if she simply faded into the background, instead of taking on a major role? He thought of the powerful bridegroom's elderly grandparents and how they might react if they realised that this was the same woman who had massaged her own peaking nipples, while wearing a dishevelled schoolgirl hockey kit. His mouth hardened. How much would it take to persuade her that she was persona non grata?

He flickered his sister a brief smile. 'Why don't you let Alannah and I have a word or two in private, *mia sorella*? And let's see if we can sort out this matter to everyone's satisfaction.'

Michela gave her friend a questioning look, but Alannah nodded.

'It's okay,' she said. 'You're quite safe to leave me alone with your brother, Michela—I'm sure he doesn't bite.'

Niccolò stiffened as Michela left the suite and his unwanted feeling of desire escalated into a dark and unremitting tide. He wondered if Alannah had made that remark to be deliberately provocative. He would certainly like to bite *her*. He'd like to sink his teeth into that slender neck and suck hungrily on that soft and creamy skin.

Her eyes were fixed on him—with that infuriating look of mild amusement still lingering in their smoky depths.

'So come on, then, Niccolò,' she said insouciantly. 'Do your worst. Why don't you get whatever is bugging you off your chest so that we can clear the air and give your sister the kind of wedding she deserves?'

'At least we are agreed on something,' he snapped. 'My sister does deserve a perfect wedding—one which will not involve a woman who will attract all the wrong kind of publicity. You have always been wild—even before you decided to strip for the cameras. And I don't think it's acceptable for every man at the ceremony to be mentally undressing the bridesmaid, instead of concentrating on the solemn vows being made between the bride and groom.'

'For someone who seems to have spent all his life avoiding commitment, I applaud your sudden dedication to the marriage service.' Her cool smile didn't slip. 'But I don't think most men are as obsessed with my past as you are.'

'You think I'm obsessed by your past?' His voice hardened. 'Oh, but you flatter yourself if you imagine that I've given you anything more than a fleeting thought in the years since you led my sister astray.' His gaze moved over her and he wondered if the lie showed in his face because he had never forgotten her, nor the effect she'd had on him. For a long time he had dreamt of her soft body and her sweet kiss— before waking up in a cold sweat as he remembered what he had nearly done to her. 'I thought you were out of her life,' he said. 'Which is where I would prefer you to stay.'

Calmly, Alannah returned his stare and told herself not to react, no matter what the provocation. Didn't matter how angry he got, she would just blank it. She'd seen enough of the world to know that remaining calm—or, at least, *appearing* to—was the most effective weapon in dealing with an adversary. And Niccolò da Conti was being *very* adversarial.

She knew he blamed her for being a bad influence on his beloved sister, so maybe she shouldn't be surprised that he still seemed to bear a grudge. She remembered reading something about him in the press—about him not being the kind of man who forgot easily. Just as he wasn't the kind of man who was easily forgotten, that was for sure. He wore his wealth lightly; his power less so. He could silence a room by entering it. He could make a woman look at him and want him, even if he was currently staring at her as if she were something which had just crawled out from underneath a rock. What right did he have to look at her like that, after all these years? Because she'd once done something which had appalled his straight-laced sensibilities—something she'd lived to regret ever since? She was a different person now and he had no right to judge her.

Yet it was working, wasn't it? The contempt in his eyes was curiously affecting. That cold black light was threatening to destabilise a poise she'd spent years trying to perfect. And if she wasn't careful, he would try to crush her. *So tell him to keep his outdated opinions to himself. Tell him you're not interested in what he has to say.*

But her indignation was beginning to evaporate, because he was loosening the top button of his shirt and drawing attention to his body. Was he doing that on purpose? she wondered weakly, hating the way her stomach had suddenly turned to liquid. Was he deliberately reminding her of a potent sexuality which had once blown her away?

She became aware that her heart was pounding like mad and that her cheeks had grown hot. She might not like him. She might consider him the most controlling person she'd ever met—but that didn't stop her from wanting him in a way she'd never wanted anyone else. Didn't seem to matter how many times she tried to block out what had happened, or tried to play it down—it made no difference. All they'd shared had been one dance and one kiss—but it had been the most erotic experience of her life and she'd never forgotten it. It had made every other man she'd met seem as insubstantial as a shadow when the fierce midday sun moved over it. It had made every other kiss seem about as exciting as kissing your teddy bear.

She ran her gaze over him, wishing he were one of those men who had developed a soft paunch in the intervening years, or that his jaw had grown slack and jowly. But not Niccolò. No way. He still had the kind of powerful physique which looked as if he could fell a tree with the single stroke of an axe. He still had the kind of looks which made people turn their heads and stare. His rugged features stopped short of being classically beautiful, but his lips looked as if they had been made with kissing in mind—even if their soft sensuality was at odds with the hostile glitter in his eyes.

She hadn't seen him for ten years and ten years could be a lifetime. In that time she'd achieved a notoriety she couldn't seem to shake off, no matter how much she tried. She'd grown used to men treating her as an object—their eyes fixed firmly on her generous breasts whenever they were talking to her.

In those ten years she'd seen her mother get sick

and die and had woken up the day after the funeral to realise she was completely alone in the world. And that had been when she'd sat down and taken stock of her life. She'd realised that she had to walk away and leave the tawdry world of glamour modelling behind. She had reached out to try something new and it hadn't been easy, but she had tried. She was still trying—still dreaming of the big break, just like everyone else. Still trying to bolster up her fragile ego and hold her head up high and make out she was strong and proud, even if inside she sometimes felt as lost and frightened as a little girl. She'd made a lot of mistakes, but she'd paid for every one of them—and she wasn't going to let Niccolò da Conti dismiss her as if she were of no consequence.

And suddenly, she was finding it difficult to do 'calm', when he was staring at her in that contemptuous way. A flicker of rebellion sparked inside her as she met his disdainful gaze.

'While you, of course, are whiter than the driven snow?' she questioned sarcastically. 'The last thing I read was that you were dating some Norwegian banker, who you then dumped in the most horrible way possible. Apparently, you have a reputation for doing that, Niccolò. The article quoted her as saying how cruel you'd been—though I guess that shouldn't have really surprised me.'

'I prefer to think of it as honesty rather than cruelty, Alannah,' he answered carelessly. 'Some women just can't accept that a relationship has run its natural course and I'm afraid Lise was one of them. But it's interesting to know you've been keeping tabs on me all this time.' He gave her a coolly mocking smile. 'I guess single billionaires must have a certain appeal to women like you, who would do pretty much anything for money. Tell me, do you track their progress as a gambler would study the form of the most promising horses in the field? Is that how it works?'

Alannah tensed. Now he'd made it sound as if she'd been *stalking* him. He was trying to make her feel bad about herself *and she wasn't going to let him.* 'Now who's flattering themselves?' she said. 'You're best friends with the Sultan of Qurhah, aren't you? And if you go out for dinner with royalty, then the photos tend to make it into the tabloids—along with speculation about why your date was seen sobbing outside your apartment the following morning. So please don't lecture me on morality, Niccolò—when you know nothing of my life.'

'And I would prefer to keep it that way,' he said. 'In fact, I'd like to keep you as far away from any member of the da Conti family as possible. So why don't we get down to business?'

She blinked at him, momentarily disconcerted. 'Business?'

'Sure. Don't look so startled—you're a big girl now, Alannah. You know how these things work. You and I need to have a little talk and we might as well do it in some degree of comfort.' He waved his hand in the direction of the cocktail cabinet which stood at the far end of the glittering hotel suite. 'Would you like a drink? Don't good-time girls always go for champagne? I can't guarantee a high-heeled shoe for you to sip it from, but I can vouch for an extremely good vintage.'

Don't rise to it, she told herself, before fixing a

weary smile to her lips. 'I hate to challenge your stereotype, but I'm not crazy about champagne and even if I was I certainly wouldn't want to drink it with you. That might imply a cordiality we both know doesn't exist. So why don't you say whatever it is you're determined to say? And then we can end this conversation as quickly as possible so that I can concentrate on fitting Michela's wedding gown.'

He didn't answer for a moment, but instead leaned back against one of the giant sofas and looked at her, his arms folded across his broad chest. Yet for all his supposedly casual stance, Alannah felt a chill of foreboding as his eyes met hers. There was a patina of power surrounding him which she hadn't noticed in that long-ago nightclub. There was a hardness about him which you didn't find in your average man. Suddenly he looked formidable—as if he was determined to remind her just who she was dealing with.

'I think we both know a simple way to resolve this,' he said softly. 'All you have to do is step out of the spotlight right now. Do that and there will be no problem. Michela is about to marry a very powerful man. She is about to take on an important role as a new wife. In time, she hopes to have children and her friends will be role models to them. And...'

'And?' she questioned, but she knew what was coming. It was crystal clear from the look on his face.

'You are not an appropriate role model,' he said. 'You're not the kind of woman I want fraternising with my nephews and nieces.'

Her heart was beating very fast. 'Don't you dare judge me,' she said, but her voice wasn't quite steady.

'Then why not make it easy for yourself? Tell Michela you've changed your mind about acting as her bridesmaid.'

'Too late!' Forcing herself to stay strong, she held up her palms in front of her, like a policeman stepping into the road to stop the traffic. 'I've made my own dress, which is currently swathed in plastic in my room, waiting for me to put it on just before noon tomorrow. I'm wearing scarlet silk to emphasise the wedding's winter theme,' she added chattily.

'But it's not going to happen,' he said repressively. 'Do you really think I would let it?'

For a moment Alannah felt another shimmer of doubt flicker into the equation. The quiet resolution of his voice scared her and so did the forthright expression in his eyes. Somehow he was making her feel...vulnerable. *And she wasn't going to let that happen.* Because she didn't do vulnerable. Not any more. Vulnerable got you nowhere. It made you fall down when life landed one of its killer punches and think you'd never be able to get back up again. It made you easy prey to powerful predators like Niccolò da Conti.

'How wicked you make me sound,' she said.

'Not wicked,' he corrected silkily. 'Just misguided, out-of-control and sexually precocious. And I don't want any publicity generated by the presence of *Stacked* magazine's most popular pin-up.'

'But nobody—'

'Michela has already mistakenly tried to tell me that nobody will know,' he interrupted impatiently. 'But they will. The magazines you stripped for have become collectors' items and back issues now change hands for thousands of dollars. And I've just been informed that a film of you has made its way onto YouTube, raising your public profile even further. It doesn't matter what you wear or what you don't wear—you still have the kind of body which occupies a fertile part of the male imagination. Men still look at you and find themselves thinking of one thing—and only one thing.'

Alannah tried not to cringe, but unfortunately his words struck home. Clever, cruel Niccolò had—unwittingly or not—tapped into her biggest insecurity. He made her feel like an object. Like a *thing*. Not a woman at all, but some two-dimensional image in a magazine—put there simply for men to lust over.

The person she was now wouldn't dream of letting her nipples peek out from behind her splayed fingers, while she pouted at the camera. These days she would rather die than hook her thumbs in her panties and thrust her pelvis in the direction of the lens. *But she'd needed to do it, for all kinds of reasons. Reasons the uptight Niccolò da Conti wouldn't understand in a million years.*

'You were *notorious*, Alannah,' he continued. 'And that kind of notoriety doesn't just go away. It sticks like mud.'

She looked at him in despair. He was telling *her* that? Didn't he realise that she'd been living with the consequences of that job ever since? No, of course he didn't. He saw what he wanted to see and no more—he didn't have the imagination to put himself in someone else's shoes and think what their life might be like. He was protected by his wealth and position and his arrogance.

She wanted to go up and shake *him* and tell him

to think outside the box. To wipe that judgemental look from his face and to start seeing her as a person, instead of someone who'd once behaved rashly. She could see exactly why Michela had been so scared of him when they'd been at school together. Was it any wonder that the Italian girl had rebelled from the moment he'd dropped her off at the exclusive Swiss finishing school where Alannah's mother had worked as school matron?

'The most important thing for me,' she said slowly, 'is that Michela wants me there. It's her day and she's the bride. So, short of tying me up and kidnapping me—I intend to be there tomorrow.'

'Unless we come to some kind of mutually beneficial arrangement,' he said.

'Oh?' She tilted her head. 'Tell me more.'

'Oh, come on, Alannah.' He smiled. 'You're a streetwise woman. You've been around. There must be something in your life that you'd...*like*.'

'Something in my life that I'd like?' she repeated. 'You mean like a cure for the common cold, or an alarm that doesn't make you want to smash the phone every time you hear it?'

'Very amusing. No, nothing like that.' He paused, and his black eyes glittered. 'I am a very wealthy man—and I'm willing to make it worth your while to tell Michela that you've changed your mind.'

She stared at him in disbelief.

'Let me get this straight,' she said. 'You're offering me *money* to stay away from your sister and not be her bridesmaid?'

'Why not?' He gave a cold smile. 'In my experience, if you want something badly enough you can usually get it. The tricky thing is negotiating the right price—but that is something I should imagine you're very good at.'

'But that's...bribery.'

'Try thinking of it as common sense,' he suggested softly.

She was shaking her head. 'You know, Michela used to tell me how unbelievably controlling you were,' she said. 'And part of me thought she might have been exaggerating. But now I can see that every word was true.'

'I am not seeking your approval of my character,' he clipped out. 'Just think why I'm making you this offer.'

'Because you're a control freak?'

'Because Michela means everything to me,' he said, and suddenly his voice grew harsh as he remembered how he'd fought to protect his sister from the sins of their father. *And their mother.* He thought of their flight from Sicily—his mother pregnant with Michela and not knowing what lay ahead. Niccolò had been only ten, but he had been the one everyone had relied on. He had been the man around the house. And it was hard to relinquish that kind of role or those kinds of expectations...

'Michela is the only family I have left in the world and I would do anything for her,' he ground out.

'Except give her the freedom which a woman of her age has the right to expect?' she retorted. 'Well, I'm *glad* she's had the courage to stand up to you. To maybe make you realise that you can't keep snapping your fingers and expecting everyone else to just leap to attention. I'm not going anywhere until after the wedding. Better deal with it, Niccolò.'

Their gazes clashed and Niccolò felt the flicker of something unknown as he returned her stare. Oh, but she was a one-off. She took defiance to a whole new level and made it seem erotic. She made him want to take her in his arms and dominate her—to show her that he could not and would not be thwarted. He took a step towards her and a primitive surge of pleasure rippled over him as he watched her eyes darken. Because she still wanted him, he realised. Maybe not quite as much as he wanted her—but the desire he could read in her eyes was unmistakable.

And couldn't desire be the most powerful weapon of all? Didn't sex give a man power over a woman who wanted it?

'Why don't you think about what I've said?' he suggested. 'So that by the time I see you at the pre-wedding dinner later, you'll have had the sense to change your mind about my offer.'

Her eyes narrowed. 'But...'

He raised his eyebrows. Suddenly, she didn't look quite so defiant. Suddenly she looked almost unsure of herself. 'But?'

'I...' She shrugged her shoulders. 'It's just that... well, Michela said you were probably going to skip the dinner and that we wouldn't see you until tomorrow. Something to do with a business deal. Some new apartment block you've recently built in London.'

'Is that what she said?' He smiled. 'Well, not any more. I've decided business can wait, because something much more important has come up.' There was a pause as he looked at her and suddenly it was easy to forget the pressing needs of his billionaire clients and friends. 'What is it they say? Keep your friends close but your enemies closer. And I want you *very* close for all kinds of reasons, Alannah. You'd better believe that.'

CHAPTER TWO

ALANNAH PULLED UP the zip of her cocktail dress and stared at her pale-faced reflection in the mirror. She'd tried deep breathing and she'd done a quick bout of yoga, but her hands were still trembling and she knew why. Slipping on a pair of high-heeled shoes, she felt a wave of self-recrimination washing over her.

She thought about the things Niccolò had said to her earlier. The way he'd insulted her and looked down his proud, patrician nose. He'd been judging her in the most negative way possible, but that hadn't stopped her wanting him. She shuddered. Where was the self-respect she'd worked so hard to get back? She wondered what had happened to the cool, calm Alannah who wasn't going to let him get under her skin. How had he managed to puncture her self-possession with nothing more than a heated ebony gaze, which reminded her of things she'd rather forget?

Because memory was a funny thing, that was why—and sometimes you had no control over it. It flipped and jerked and jumped around like a flapping fish on the end of a hook. It took you to places you didn't want to visit. It could make ten years seem like a minute, or a minute seem like an hour.

It could put you back inside the skin of the person you'd once been.

And suddenly she was a teenager again. Seventeen years old and about to break the rules. Off to a party wearing the make-up which her Swiss finishing school strictly forbade, when really she should have been tucked up in bed in the dormitory. Wearing a tiny little micro-mini because she had been young and carefree—because back then she hadn't realised that a woman's body could become her enemy, instead of her friend...

By rights, someone like her shouldn't have been a pupil at the exclusive all-girls academy, tucked high in the beautiful mountains of Switzerland. She wasn't rich. She wasn't well-connected. She was just the illegitimate daughter of a single-parent mother who happened to be Matron at the fancy boarding school. And while this meant that Alannah got herself a great education, her 'charity' status meant that most of the girls simply tolerated her.

Michela da Conti was different. She was the only one who had held out the hand of genuine friendship—maybe because they had something in common, despite their rich-girl/poor-girl pairing. Alannah had spent her life rebelling against her super-strict mother while Michela had known real tragedy in her short life, plus she wanted to escape the strictures of her controlling brother, Niccolò.

Their youthful rebellion usually stretched no further than going out for illicit under-age drinks in one of the nearby bars after lights-out, or hanging out of the dormitory window, trying to inhale cigarettes without being sick.

But one night they heard about a party. A glitzy twenty-first birthday celebration for one of Niccolò's godsons—which was being held in one of the neighbouring mountain valleys.

'And we're going!' declared Michela excitedly.

Alannah remembered frowning. 'But what about your brother? Won't he be there?'

'You're kidding.' Michela had given a smile of satisfaction. 'Apparently, he's miles away in some obscenely expensive resort in Barbados, with his latest ghastly supermodel girlfriend. So we're safe.'

Alannah remembered walking into the crowded room, where coloured lights were flashing and music was blaring out loudly. Her borrowed silver minidress was clinging to her body like honey and she was getting lots of requests to dance, but she turned down every one because all the boys seemed too loud and too brash to be interesting.

She did her best to enjoy herself. She sipped a soft drink and admired the snowy view. Found a sleeping kitten on her way back from the loo and spent an enjoyable ten minutes stroking its furry tummy and wishing she could go home. When eventually she went back into the main room to find Michela to suggest they got a cab back to school, she couldn't find her anywhere. So she went and stood in a quiet corner of the room, losing herself in the shadows while everyone else partied—and that was when she saw him.

Him.

She had never forgotten that moment. It was like being struck by something with no sense of warning that it was coming. As if a velvet sledgehammer had hit her very hard. She was aware that he was tall and his hair was as black as the night sky. His eyes were black too—even from this distance she could see that. He was dressed in a dark suit, which made him look outwardly sophisticated, but she could sense something *primitive* about him. There was something predatory in the gleam of his eyes, which should have scared her as he began to walk towards her, with a sense of purpose in his step.

But she wasn't scared.

It was the most illogical thought she'd ever had, but at that moment she felt as if she'd been waiting all her life for him to arrive, and here he was.

Here he was.

He looked her up and down—as if it was his right to study a strange woman as he might study a car he was thinking of buying. But surely no car would make him smile like that—a smile which seemed to come from somewhere deep inside him, one that pierced her heart and made her knees feel as if they might have difficulty supporting her.

'I think you need to dance,' he said.

'I'm not a very good dancer.'

'That's because you've never danced with me. So come here and let me teach you how.'

Later, she would remonstrate with herself at the eagerness with which she fell into his arms. At the way she let him slide his hands around her back as if she'd known him for years. His hand moved to her hair and he started stroking it and suddenly she wanted to purr as loudly as that kitten had done earlier.

They said very little. The party was too loud for conversation and, anyway, it didn't seem to be conversation which was dominating Alannah's thoughts right then. Or his. Words seemed superfluous as he pulled her closer and, although the music was fast, they danced so slowly that they barely moved. Their bodies felt as if they were glued together and Alannah almost wept with the sheer pleasure of it all. Did he sense her enjoyment? Was that why he dipped his mouth to her ear, so that she could feel the warmth of his breath fanning her skin?

'You,' he said, his velvety voice underpinned with an accent which she recognised as Sicilian, 'are very beautiful.'

Wasn't it funny how some people you just seemed to spark off? So that she—inexperienced and raw as she was—didn't respond in a conventional way. She didn't blush and tell him she wasn't beautiful at all— but instead came out with something which sounded almost slick.

'And you,' she cooed back, looking straight into his black eyes, 'are very handsome.'

He smiled. 'A perfect match, then?'

She tipped her head back. 'Aren't you getting a little ahead of yourself?'

'Probably.' He leaned forward, so that her face was bathed in the dark spotlight of his gaze. 'Especially as we haven't even kissed. Don't you think that's a shocking omission, my beauty? So shocking that I think we ought to remedy it right now.'

She remembered the way her heart had crashed loudly against her ribcage. The way her mouth had dried with anticipation and the words had just come tumbling out of her mouth. 'Who says I'm going to kiss you?'

'I do.'

And he did.

In that shadowy corner of some anonymous house in the Swiss mountains, while outside flakes of snow floated past the window like big, white feathers, he kissed her.

He kissed her so intensely that Alannah thought she might faint. He kissed her for so long that she wanted him never to stop. It was like that pile of bone-dry sticks she'd once built on a long-ago holiday to Ireland—she remembered the way they'd combusted into flames the moment her aunt had put a match to them. Well, it was a bit like that now.

She was on fire.

His thumb brushed over her breast and Alannah wriggled with excitement. Because surely this was what she had been made for—to stand in this man's arms and be touched by him. To have him look at her as if she were the most beautiful woman in the world. He deepened the kiss to one of added intimacy and as he pushed his thigh between hers the atmosphere suddenly changed. It became charged. She could feel the flood of liquid heat to her groin and the sudden, almost painful hardening of her nipples as they pushed insistently against his chest. His breath was unsteady as he pulled away from her and there was a primitive emotion on his face which she didn't recognise.

'We'd better think about moving somewhere more comfortable,' he said roughly. 'Somewhere with a bed.'

Alannah never had a chance to reply because suddenly the mood was broken by some kind of commotion at the door. She felt him tense as Michela burst into the room with snow melting on her raven hair, and the guilty look on her friend's face when she saw Niccolò told its own story.

It was unfortunate that Michela was surrounded by the miasma of sickly-sweet marijuana smoke—and even more unfortunate when Niccolò's discreet enquiries the next day yielded up the information that both girls were already on a formal warning from the school. A small matter of the building's elaborate fire-alarm system having been set off by the two of them hanging out of a dormitory window, smoking.

Alannah would never forget the look of passion dying on Niccolò's face, only to see it being replaced with one of disgust as he looked at her. She remembered wanting to wither beneath it.

'You are my sister's friend?' he questioned incredulously. 'Her *school friend*?'

'Y-yes.'

'How old are you?'

'Seventeen.'

All the colour drained from his face and he looked as if she'd hit him. 'So Michela associates with a *puttana*, does she?' he hissed. 'A cheap little tart who puts out for strangers at parties.'

'I d-don't remember you objecting,' she stammered, stung into defending herself, even if deep down she felt she had no real defence to offer.

'No man objects when a woman offers herself to him on a plate like that,' he snapped.

The following day he had withdrawn Michela from the school and shortly afterwards the head teacher had summoned Alannah and her mother to her office. The head had clearly been furious at the prospect of having to say goodbye to Niccolò da Conti's generous donations to the school. She had told Alannah that her behaviour was unacceptable and her mother had pre-empted the inevitable expulsion by offering up her resignation.

'I'm not having my girl scapegoated by some rich financier,' she'd said fiercely. 'If you're going to heap all the blame on her, then this is not the kind of school for her.'

Of course, that was not an end to it—merely the beginning of a nightmare which put the whole Niccolò incident to the back of her mind.

But she'd never grassed up Michela and Michela had remained loyal to her ever since.

Her thoughts cleared and she saw her friend looking at her in the dressing-table mirror, her face still glowing from her pre-wedding facial, and Alannah sighed as she met Michela's questioning gaze. 'Maybe it would be better if I just bowed out, if it's going to cause a massive row between you and your brother. I'll just stand at the back like everyone else and throw rose petals. I can live with that.'

Michela glared as she put her hairbrush down.

'And let Niccolò have his own way? I don't think so. You've been the best of friends to me, Alannah—and I want you there. In fact, it'll probably do Niccolò good on all kinds of levels. I've never heard *anyone* speak to him the way you do.' She smirked. 'Nobody else would dare.'

Alannah wondered what Michela would say if she realised how much of her reaction to her powerful brother was bravado. That her feelings for him were... *complicated*. Would she be shocked if she knew the truth? That she only had to look at him to want to rip the shirt from his body and feast her eyes on all that silken olive flesh? That somehow he brought out a wildness in her which frightened her. Which she knew was wrong. And not only wrong…she knew only too well that those supposedly seamless sexual fantasies were nothing but an illusion.

She forced a smile. 'Okay, if you insist…it'll be business as usual. In which case, we'd better get going. I know it's traditional for the bride to keep her groom waiting on the big day, but not on the eve-of-wedding dinner!'

They took the elevator down to the iconic Midnight Room, where a large clock was set permanently at the witching hour. It was a spectacular party room designed by Emma Constantinides, the hotel owner's wife—and had won countless industry prizes since its opening. Circular tables had been set for dinner and the dark velvet ceiling was punctured with tiny lights, so that it resembled a star-filled sky. In the silvery light from hundreds of candles, people in evening dress stood drinking champagne as the scent of dark blue hyacinths wafted through the air.

A roar of delight greeted the bride-to-be's appearance and Alannah leaned forward to whisper in Michela's ear as people began to surge towards them. 'You go and sparkle,' she said. 'Anything you need me to check?'

Michela shook her head. She had already spotted Lucas on the opposite side of the room, talking to his mother. 'No. You go and sparkle too,' she said. 'And for goodness' sake, have a very large cocktail before we sit down to dinner. You look completely washed out, Alannah.'

But Alannah refused a drink. A drink on an empty stomach was a recipe for disaster and hers was already in knots. All she had to do was to get through the next thirty-six hours without crumbling, and surely she could do that.

And then she looked around the room and saw Niccolò—and every empowering thought flew straight from her mind as her gaze focused on him.

He was standing talking to a blonde whose sequined dress left little to the imagination and Alannah found herself thinking that he didn't seem to have a problem with *that*. The woman was gazing up at him and nodding intently, as if nothing but pearls of wisdom were falling from those cruel and kissable lips. There were other women clustering nearby, too—as if he were a dark shark and they were all hungry little pilot fish, just waiting for whatever scraps he cared to leave for them.

He lifted his head as if he had sensed her watching him—glancing across the room to where she stood. And suddenly it was too late to look away. His gaze captured hers and held it and it felt as if some fierce dark light were piercing through her skin. She felt sensitive. Exposed and raw. Terrified he would see through to the dark mass of insecurities hidden beneath her cool exterior, she tried to look away, but she couldn't. *She couldn't.* He seemed to be drawing her in by the force of his formidable will.

Desperately, she tried to compose herself. To concentrate on something other than how beautifully the dark suit caressed his hard body, but she failed at that, too. Instead she found herself staring at the snowy edge of his dinner-shirt and the way his olive skin gleamed like burnished gold above it.

He bent his head to say something to the blonde, who turned to look at her, and Alannah thought she saw faint surprise clouding the other woman's eyes. Had her uncomfortable stance given her away—making the woman guess that she was the outsider here?

She forced herself to turn away to talk to some of the other guests, who seemed genuinely charmed by her English accent, and for a while she allowed herself to relax before the bell rang for dinner. But a glance at the seating plan showed her that she was next to Niccolò—*of course she was,* for hadn't Michela made it clear that she wanted the two of them to get along better? She wondered when her friend was going to realise that it simply wasn't going to happen. Or at least, not in this lifetime. Her heart began thumping painfully as she made her way towards the top table.

She felt his presence behind her even before his shadow fell over the table. The palms of her hands were clammy and the race of her heart was thready, but somehow she managed to fix a wide smile to her lips as she turned to look at him.

'Niccolò!' she said brightly.

'Just the person you wanted to sit beside, right?'

'How did you guess?' Solely for the benefit of the other guests, she maintained that brittle rictus of a smile. 'You were right at the top of my list.'

But Alannah tensed as he leaned forward to kiss her on both cheeks, just as he would have done to any other female guest. She wondered if any other female guest would have reacted the way she did, with a pulse which was threatening to rocket out of control and a desire to tip her head up so that his mouth would meet hers, instead of grazing the innocent surface of her cheek. She found herself longing to reach up to touch that hard, chiselled jaw and to feel it scrape against her fingertips. She wanted to press her lips against his ear and kiss it. And how crazy was that? How could you want a man so much when you didn't even *like* him?

Stop it, she told herself as he pulled out her chair with an exaggerated courtesy, which seemed to be at odds with the mockery gleaming from his eyes. Did he know what kind of effect he had on her? Did he realise that her legs were weak and her breasts growing heavy? He sat down next to her and she could smell his warm, male flesh—as subtle and spicy as sandalwood—and all she wanted to do was to breathe it in. Reaching out, she picked up her champagne flute and took a gulp.

She could feel him watching as she drank the cold, fizzy wine but the champagne tasted as sour as a remedy you might take for an upset stomach. She put down her glass and looked at him, because they couldn't go on like this. Not with a whole day and a half to get through.

'I think Michela has sat us together deliberately,' she said.

He raised his eyebrows. 'Because?'

'I think she's hoping that we're going to declare some sort of truce.'

'Why—are we engaged in some sort of battle?'

'Please don't be disingenuous, Niccolò. You know we are. We've done nothing but argue since we reconnected.' She shrugged. 'And while that seems to be what you seem to want—I'd prefer it, and your sister would prefer it, if we could manage to be non-confrontational. At least, in public.'

Niccolò met her denim-blue eyes and gave a small dissenting shake of his head—thinking how wrong she'd got it. Because battle was the last thing he wanted. His needs around Alannah Collins were much more fundamental. He might even have contemplated a more conventional route by asking her out on a date, if she hadn't been the kind of woman he despised.

Yet there was nothing of the precocious teenager or sexy glamour model about her tonight. The image she presented was almost *demure*. Her navy silk dress was high-necked and the hemline showed nothing more than an couple of inches of slender knee. A small, glittering brooch in the shape of a fluttering moth was her only jewellery. Her most magnificent assets—the breasts which had once so captured the imagination of the British public—were only hinted at and certainly not on show. All he could see was the occasional glimpse of a soft curve as the material brushed against them. He swallowed. Was she aware that it was just as provocative to conceal something, as to reveal it?

Of course she was.

Trading on her own sexuality had been her stock-in-trade, hadn't it? She knew everything there was to know about how to pull in the punters and leave them slavering for more.

Shaking out his napkin, he placed it in his lap and scowled, recalling the first time he'd seen her at his godson's birthday party.

He remembered looking in amazement at the silver dress, which had clung to her curvy body like melted butter, and thinking that he'd never seen anyone looking quite so alluring. Had he been frustrated? Too long without a woman? Unlikely. All he knew was that he hadn't been able to tear his eyes away from her.

The look which had passed between them had been timeless. The lust which had overwhelmed him had been almost tangible. He had never experienced anything like it in his life—not before, nor since. The hardness at his groin had been almost unbearable as he had danced with her. Something elemental had caught him in its grip and he'd felt almost...*lost.* The dance had been simply a formality—paving the way for their first kiss. He had kissed her for a long time, tempted by a need to pull her into a dark and anonymous corner and just *take* her. And even though he detested being out of control...even though his own history had warned him this was not the way to go— it hadn't been enough to deter him from acting on it.

He had been just about to drive her back to his hotel, when there had been some sort of commotion by the door. He remembered turning to see Michela giggling as she'd entered the room, accompanied by a group of boys. His *sister.* Large flakes of snow had been melting on her raven hair and her look of guilt when she had seen him had told its own story.

And that was when Niccolò had discovered that Alannah Collins wasn't some twenty-something party guest, but the teenage best friend of his only sister. A wild-child who had been threatening to ruin Michela's reputation and bring shame on the da Conti name, after he'd spent years meticulously dragging it from the mud.

Was it any wonder that he despised her?

Was it any wonder that he despised himself, knowing what he had nearly done to her?

What he still wanted to do to her.

He leaned back in his chair, paying little attention to the plates of smoked salmon which were being placed in front of them. 'Did you ever tell Michela what happened between us?' he questioned suddenly.

She stiffened a little before turning to look at him, her eyes narrowing warily. 'But nothing did happen.'

'Oh, come on.' He gave a harsh laugh. 'It might as well have done. It would have done, if my sister hadn't arrived. I've never had a dance quite so erotic as the one I had with you. It was a dance which was headed straight for the bedroom.'

'Oh, for heaven's sake—'

'Does Michela realise that you would have spent the night with me if she hadn't turned up when she did?'

'You can't know that.'

'Yes, I can. And so can you. Why don't you try being honest with yourself for once, Alannah?' He leaned forward and his voice roughened. 'I know enough about women to realise when they want a man to make love to them—and you were screaming out to have me do it to you that night.'

'Really?' She took a nervous sip of her drink.

'And you've avoided answering my question,' he persisted. 'What exactly did you tell Michela?'

There was a pause. 'I didn't tell her anything.'

'Why not?'

Alannah shrugged, reluctant to admit the truth—that she'd been too ashamed of her own reaction to want to acknowledge it to anyone and certainly not to her best friend. That she'd felt dirty and cheap. Michela had warned her that her big brother was a 'player'. That he changed his women nearly as often as he changed his shirts. She remembered the two of them agreeing that any woman who went out with a man like him was *sad*. But she'd nearly been one of those women, hadn't she? Because he was right. If Michela hadn't walked in right then, she would have...

Briefly, she let her eyes close. She'd been so in thrall to him that he probably could have taken her outside and taken her virginity pressed up against a cold and snowy tree. She had certainly been up for going back to his hotel with him.

She opened her eyes and looked at him. 'Why not? Because even though Michela has always thought you a total control freak, she absolutely idolised you—and I knew you were the only family she had. It wasn't for me to disillusion her by telling her that you'd been hitting on her best friend.'

'Hitting on her best friend?' He gave a cynical smile. 'Oh, please. Unfortunately, I didn't realise I was dealing with *jailbait* at the time. You kept that one crucial fact to yourself.'

'Is that why you got me expelled?' she said, without missing a beat.

He shook his head. 'I didn't mention your name when I withdrew Michela from the school.'

Her eyes narrowed. 'Are you serious?'

He shrugged. 'There was no need. I thought I was removing Michela from your bad example—what I didn't realise was that you were going to continue the friendship behind my back.'

Alannah ran her fingertip down over her champagne glass, leaving behind a transparent stripe in the condensation. 'But all that happened a long time ago,' she said slowly.

'I guess it did.' He leaned back in his chair. 'And since your role seems to be non-negotiable, I guess I'm just going to have to be nice to you.'

'Is that possible?'

'Me being nice?' He watched the golden flicker of candlelight playing on her pale skin. 'You don't think so?'

'Not really. I think it would be like someone hand-rearing a baby tiger and then expecting it to lap contentedly from a saucer of milk when it reaches adulthood. Naïve and unrealistic.'

'And nobody could ever accuse you of that.'

'Certainly not someone with as cutting a tongue as you, Niccolò.'

He laughed, his gaze drifting over fingers which he noticed were bare of rings. 'So what has been happening to you in the last ten years? Bring me up to speed.'

Alannah didn't answer for a moment. He didn't want to know that her life had imploded like a dark star when her mother had died and that for a long time she had felt completely empty. Men like Niccolò weren't interested in other people's sadness or ambition. They asked polite questions at dinner parties because that was what they had been taught to do—and all they required was something fairly meaningless in response.

She shook her head at the waitress who was offering her a basket heaped with different breads. 'I'm an interior designer these days.'

'Oh?' He waited while the pretty waitress stood close to him for slightly longer than was necessary, before reluctantly moving away. 'How did that happen? Did you wake up one morning and decide you were an expert on soft furnishings?'

'That's a very patronising comment.'

'I have experience of interior designers,' he said wryly. 'And of rich, bored women who decide to set themselves up as experts.'

'Well, I'm neither rich, nor bored. And I think you'll find there's more to the job than that. I studied fashion at art school and was planning to make dresses, but the fashion world is notoriously tough—and it's difficult to get funding.' Especially when you had the kind of past which meant that people formed negative judgements about you.

'So what did you do?'

'I worked for a big fashion chain for a while,' she continued, pushing her fork aimlessly around her plate. 'Before I realised that what I was best at was putting together a "look". I liked putting colours and fabrics together and creating interesting interiors. I spent a few years working for a large interiors company to gain experience and recently I took the plunge and set up on my own.'

'And are you any good?' he questioned. 'How come I've never heard of you?'

'I think I'm good—have a look at my website and decide for yourself,' she said. 'And the reason you haven't heard of me is because there are a million other designers out there. I'm still waiting for my big break.'

'And your topless modelling career?' he questioned idly. 'Did that fall by the wayside?'

Alannah tried not to flinch, terrified he would see how much his question had hurt. For a minute back then she'd actually thought they were sticking to their truce and talking to each other like two normal human beings. 'This is you being "nice", is it, Niccolò? Behaving as if I was something you'd found on the sole of your shoe?'

His eyes didn't leave her face. 'All I'm doing is asking a perfectly legitimate question about your former career.'

'Which you can't seem to do without that expression of disgust on your face.'

'Wouldn't anyone be disgusted?' he demanded hotly. 'Isn't the idea of a woman peddling her flesh to the highest bidder abhorrent to any man with a shred of decency in his bones? Although I suspect the end-product must have been spectacular.' There was a pause before he spoke. 'Alannah Collins *shaking her booty.*'

His last few words were murmured—and Alannah thought how unexpected the colloquialism sounded when spoken in that sexy Sicilian accent of his. But his words reminded her that what you saw wasn't necessarily what you got. Despite his cosmopolitan appearance and lifestyle, Niccolò da Conti was as traditional as they came. His views and his morals came straight from another age. No wonder his sister had been so terrified of him. No wonder she'd gone off the rails when she had been freed from his claustro-phobic presence and judgemental assessment.

'Those photographs were stills,' she said tonelessly. 'I never *shook* anything.'

'Ah, but surely you're just splitting hairs.' He gave a dangerous smile, his finger idly circling the rim of his untouched champagne glass. 'Unless you're try-ing to tell me that cupping your breasts and simulat-ing sexual provocation for the camera while wearing a school uniform is a respectable job for a woman?'

Alannah managed to twist a sliver of smoked salmon onto the end of her fork, but the food never made it to her mouth. 'Shall I tell you why I did that job?'

'Easy money, I'm guessing.'

She put the fork back down. Oh, what was the point? she thought tiredly. He didn't *care* what had motivated her. He had judged her—he was still judg-ing her—on the person she appeared to be. Someone who had danced too intimately with a stranger at a party. Someone who had gone off the rails with his beloved sister. Someone who had discovered that the only way to keep hope alive had been by taking off her clothes...

Who could blame him for despising her—for not realising that she was so much more than that?

She dabbed at her lips with her napkin. 'On second thoughts, I don't think polite interaction is going to be possible after all. There's actually too much his-tory between us.'

'Or not enough?' he challenged and suddenly his voice grew silky. 'Don't you think it might be a good idea to forge some new memories, Alannah? Something which might cancel out all the frustrations of the past?'

Alannah stiffened. Was he suggesting what she *thought* he was suggesting? Was he *flirting* with her? She swallowed. And if he were? If he were, she needed to nip it in the bud. To show him she respected herself and her body.

She slanted him a smile. 'I don't think that's going to happen. I think we need to avoid each other as much as possible. We'll support Michela all the way and try not to let our mutual animosity show, but nothing more than that. So why don't you do me a favour and talk to the woman on your other side? She's been trying to get your attention since you first sat down and she's very beautiful.' She picked up her wine glass and took a sip, her eyes surveying him coolly over the rim. 'I'm surprised you hadn't noticed that, Niccolò.'

CHAPTER THREE

IT WAS THE worst night he'd had in a long time, or maybe it was just that Niccolò couldn't remember ever losing sleep over a woman before. He lay tossing and turning in the king-size bed of his hotel room, trying to convince himself that Alannah had been right and the less time they spent together, the better. But every time he thought about distancing himself from those denim-blue eyes and that pouting, provocative mouth he felt an uncomfortable ache deep inside him.

What was the matter with him?

Kicking away the rumpled sheet, he told himself she wasn't his kind of woman—that she represented everything he despised in a sometimes trashy and disposable society.

Abandoning all further attempts to sleep, he dealt with his emails and spoke to his assistant in London, who informed him that Alekto Sarantos was still unhappy with the interior of the penthouse suite. The Greek billionaire had let it be known that the apartment's design was too 'bland' for his tastes and, despite a close association going back years, he was now considering pulling out of the deal and buying in Paris instead. Niccolò silently cursed his temperamental friend as he terminated the phone-call and wondered how soon he could decently leave after the wedding to return to work.

Pulling on his gym gear, he went for a run in Central Park, where the bare trees were etched dramatically against the winter sky. Despite his restless night and the fact that little was in bloom, his senses seemed unusually receptive to the beauty which surrounded him on this cold winter morning. There were ducks and gulls on the lakes and woodpeckers were tapping in the trees. Other runners were already out pounding the paths and an exquisite-looking blonde smiled hopefully at him, slowing down as he approached. But he didn't even bother giving her a second look. Her eyes were glacial green, not denim blue—and it was that particular hue which had been haunting his sleep last night.

The run took the edge off his restlessness, even if it didn't quell it completely, and after he'd showered and dressed he found a series of increasingly frantic texts from his sister queuing up on his smartphone. The final one was followed by a wobbly voicemail message, demanding to know where he was.

He went along the corridor and knocked at her door—stupidly unprepared for the sight of Alannah opening the door, even though he'd known she was sharing a suite with his sister. He felt almost *high* as he looked at her and could feel the aching throb of longing which stabbed at his groin. She was wearing a denim shirt-dress which matched her eyes and a tiny ladybird brooch which twinkled red and black on the high collar. For a moment it occurred to him that she was dressed as sedately as a schoolteacher and he watched as a complicated series of expressions flitted across her face as she looked at him, before producing a smile which was clearly forced.

'Hi,' she said.

'Hi.' He tried his own version of that fake smile. 'Sleep well?'

She raised her eyebrows. 'You're here to enquire how I slept?'

No, I'm here because I'd like to take your panties down and put my tongue between your thighs. He shrugged. 'Michela has been bombarding my phone with texts. Is she here?'

'She's...' cocking her head in the direction of one of the closed doors behind her, she pulled a face '...in the bathroom.'

'Is something wrong?'

'She's broken a nail.'

He frowned. 'Is that supposed to be some kind of a joke?'

'No, Niccolò, it's not a joke. It's the finger her wedding ring will go on and everyone will notice. To a bride who's just hours away from the ceremony, something like this is nothing short of a catastrophe. I've called the manicurist, who's on her way up.'

'First World problems,' he said caustically. 'So everything is under control?'

'Well, that depends how you look at it.' She met his gaze and seemed to be steeling herself to say something. 'Her nerves aren't helped by the worry that you're going to lose your temper at some point today.'

'What makes her think that?'

'Heaven only knows,' she said sarcastically, 'when you have a reputation for being so mild-mannered and accommodating. Could it have something to do with the fact that you and I were at loggerheads throughout dinner last night, and she noticed?'

He raised his eyebrows. 'So what does she want us to do—kiss and make up?'

'Hardly,' she snapped. 'That might be stretching credibility a little too far.'

'Oh, I think I could manage to put on a convincing enough performance,' he drawled. 'How about you?'

So she *hadn't* been imagining it last night. Alannah stiffened. He really *was* flirting. And she was going to have to put on the performance of a lifetime if she wanted to convince him that it wasn't working.

She raised her eyebrows. 'So can I tell Michela that you're planning to be a good boy today? Do you think you're a competent enough actor to simulate enjoyment and behave yourself for the duration of the wedding?'

'I don't usually have to simulate anything—and I've never been called a *good boy* in my life,' he answered softly. 'But if Michela wants reassurance that I'm going to behave myself, then tell her yes. I will be extremely virtuous. And I will be back here at three, to take you both down to the wedding.'

Alannah gave a brief nod and her cool, careful smile didn't slip until she had shut the door on him, though her pulse was pounding loudly.

At least an air of calm had descended by the time the manicurist arrived to repair the tattered nail and the mood was elevated still further as Alannah helped Michela slide into her delicate white gown. Because this was *her* territory, she reminded herself fiercely.

She was proud of the dress she'd made for the bride and she wasn't going to let Niccolò da Conti whittle away at her confidence.

Her movements became sure and confident as she smoothed down the fine layers of tulle and soon she felt like herself again—Alannah Collins, who was living life according to her own rules, and ignoring the false perceptions of other people.

But the moment Niccolò arrived all that composure deserted her. She was aware of his piercing gaze as he watched her adjusting the floral circlet which held Michela's veil in place and it was difficult to keep her fingers steady. She could feel his dark eyes moving over her and the only comfort she got was by reminding herself that after this day was over, she need never see him again.

So why did that make her heart plummet, as if someone had dropped it to the bottom of a lift-shaft?

'You look beautiful, *mia sorella*,' he said, and Michela gave a smile of delight as she did a twirl.

'*Do* I?'

'Indeed you do.' His voice was indulgent. 'Lucas is a very lucky man.'

'Well, I have Alannah to thank for my appearance,' said Michela brightly. 'She's the one who made the dress. It's gorgeous, isn't it, Niccolò?'

Alannah wanted to tell her friend to stop trying so hard. To tell her that she and her brother were never going to achieve anything more than a forced civility. But she maintained the fiction necessary to soothe the bride's frazzled nerves by smiling at him in what she hoped looked like a friendly way.

'It is indeed a very beautiful dress,' he agreed

softly, his eyes gleaming out a silent message which she didn't dare analyse.

Alannah tried to relax as she handed Michela her bouquet and the three of them made their way to the Pembroke's celebrated wedding room, where the assembled guests were waiting. A harpist began to play and Alannah saw the sudden look of tension which hardened Niccolò's features into a grim mask as he gave his sister away to be married.

Maybe he just didn't like weddings, she thought.

She tried not to stare at him as the vows were made and to ignore the women who were clearly trying to catch his eye. And after the rings had been exchanged, Alannah tried to be the best guest she possibly could. She chatted to the groom's sister and offered to suggest some new colour schemes for her house in Gramercy Park. After the wedding breakfast, she took time to play with several of the frilly-dressed little girls from Lucas's huge extended family. And when they were all worn out, she lined them all up to twist their long hair into intricate styles, which made them squeal with delight.

By the time the tables had been cleared and the band had struck up for the first dance, Alannah felt able to relax at last. Her duties had been performed to everyone's satisfaction and the wedding had gone off without a hitch. Drink in hand, she stood on the edge of the dance-floor and watched Michela dancing in the arms of Lucas—soft white tulle floating around her slender body and a dreamy smile on her face as she looked up at her new husband.

Alannah felt her heart contract and wished it wouldn't. She didn't want to feel *wistful,* not today—

of all days. To wonder why some people found love easy while others seemed to have a perpetual struggle with it. Or to question why all that stuff had never happened to her.

'How come I always find you standing alone on the dance-floor?'

Alannah's heart clenched at the sound of Niccolò's Sicilian accent, but she didn't turn round. She just carried on standing there until he walked up to stand beside her.

'I'm just watching the happy couple,' she said conversationally.

He followed the direction of her gaze and for a moment they stood in silence as Lucas whirled Michela round in his arms.

'Do you think they'll stay happy?' he asked suddenly.

The question surprised her. 'Don't you?'

'If they are contented to work with what they've got and to build on it, then, yes, they have a chance. But if they start to believe in all the hype...' His voice grew hard. 'If they want stardust and spangles, then they will be disappointed.'

'You obviously don't rate marriage very highly.'

'I don't. The odds against it are too high. It's a big gamble—and I am not a gambling man.'

'And love?' she questioned as she turned at last to look at him. 'What about love?'

His mouth hardened and for a moment she thought she saw something bleak flaring at the depths of his black eyes.

'Love is a weakness,' he said bitterly, 'which brings out the worst in people.'

'That's a little—'

'Dance with me,' he said suddenly, his words cutting over hers, and Alannah tensed as his fingers curled over her bare arm.

They were a variation on the words he'd spoken all those years ago. Words which had once turned her head. But she was older now and hopefully wiser— or maybe she was just disillusioned. She no longer interpreted his imperious command as masterful— but more as an arrogant demonstration of the control which was never far from the surface.

She lifted her face to his. 'Do I get a choice in the matter?'

'No.' Removing the glass from her hand, he placed it on the tray of a passing waitress, before sliding his hand proprietorially around her waist and propelling her towards the dance floor. 'I'm afraid you don't.'

She told herself that she didn't have to do this. She could excuse herself and walk away. Because he was unlikely to start behaving like a cave-man by dragging her onto the dance-floor—not with all his new in-laws around.

Except that she left it a split second too long and suddenly it was too late for objections. Suddenly, she was on the dance-floor and his arms were round her waist and the worst thing of all was that she *liked* it. She liked it way too much.

'You can't do this, Niccolò,' she said breathlessly. 'It's over-the-top alpha behaviour.'

'But I just can't help myself,' he said mockingly. 'I'm an over-the-top alpha man. Surely you knew that, Alannah.'

Oh, yes. She knew that. A block of stone would

have known that. Alannah swallowed because his hands were tightening around her waist and making her feel there was no place else she would rather be. She told herself it would cause a scene and reflect badly on both of them if she pulled away from him. *So endure it. One dance and it will all be over.*

She tried to relax as they began to move in time with the music and for a while they said nothing. But it wasn't easy to pretend that it meant nothing to be wrapped in his arms again. Actually, it was close to impossible. His body was so hard and his arms were so strong. His unique scent of sandalwood and raw masculinity seemed to call out to something deep inside her—to touch her on a subliminal level which no one else had even come close to. She could hear the thunder of her heart as he lowered his head to her ear and even his voice seemed to flood over her like velvety-dark chocolate.

'Enjoying yourself?' he said.

She swallowed. 'I was before you forced me into this farce of pretending we have a civilised enough relationship to be dancing together.'

'But surely you can't have any complaints about what we're doing, *mia tentatrice.* Aren't I behaving like a perfect gentleman?'

'Not with...' Her words tailed away, because now he had moved his hands upwards and his fingers were spanning her back. She could feel their imprint burning through the delicate material of her bridesmaid dress and her throat constricted.

'With what?'

'You're holding me too tightly,' she croaked.

'I'm barely holding you at all.'

'You are a master of misinterpretation.'

'I am a master of many things,' came the silken boast, 'but misinterpretation wouldn't have been top of my list.'

She looked up from where she had been staring resolutely at his black tie and forced herself to meet the mocking light in his eyes. 'Why are you doing this?' she whispered.

'Dancing with you? Isn't it customary for the brother of the bride to dance with the bridesmaid at some point—particularly if both of them are single? Or were you holding out for the best man?'

'I'm not holding out for anyone. And I don't remember telling you I was single.'

'But you are, aren't you? And if you're not, then you might as well be.' He met her eyes. 'Because you are responding like a woman who hasn't been touched by a man for a very long time.'

She was tempted to snap back at him with indignation, but how could she? Because he was right. It *was* a long time since she had been touched by a man. It was a long time since she had danced with a man too, and it had never felt like this. Not with anyone. *It had only ever felt like this with him.*

'I don't understand what it is you want,' she said. 'Why you're dancing with me. Taunting me. Trying to get underneath my skin. Especially when you don't even *like* me—and the feeling is mutual.'

He pulled her closer. 'But not liking doesn't stop us *wanting*, does it, Alannah? Desire doesn't require affection in order to flourish. On the contrary, sometimes it works better without it. Don't you find that, *mia tentatrice*?' He stroked a reflective finger along her waist. 'That sex can be *so* much more exciting when there is a frisson of animosity between a man and a woman?'

Her skin still tingling from the lazy caress of his finger, she pulled away from him, trying to focus on the presumptuous things he was saying, rather than the way her body was reacting. 'Stop it,' she said weakly.

'But you haven't answered my question.'

'And I don't have to. Just as I don't have to stand here and take any more provocative comments. My duty dance is over.' With a monumental effort, she pulled away from him. 'Thanks for reminding me what a consummate player you are, Niccolò. And thanks for reminding me that ten years might have passed but you don't seem to have changed. You still treat the opposite sex as if—'

'I wouldn't generalise if I were you,' he interjected and now his voice was edged with steel. 'Because you have no idea how I treat women. And believe me when I tell you that I've never had any complaints.'

The sexual boast was blatant and Alannah suddenly felt as if her skin were too tight for her body. As if her flesh wanted to burst out of her bridesmaid dress. Her breasts were tingling and she knew she had to get away from him before she did something she regretted—or said something she would never live down. 'Goodnight, Niccolò,' she said, turning away and beginning to walk across the dance-floor. 'I think we can officially declare our truce to be over.'

Niccolò watched her go and felt frustration mount inside him, along with an even greater feeling of disbelief. She had gone. She had walked away with her head held high and her shoulders stiff and proud, and all his hunter instincts were aroused as he watched the retreating sway of her silk-covered bottom.

He swallowed.

He had played it wrong.

Or maybe he had just read her wrong.

She had been right. He didn't particularly like her and he certainly didn't *respect* her. But what did that have to do with anything? He still wanted her in a way he'd never wanted anyone else.

And tomorrow she would be gone. Leaving New York and going back to her life in London. And even though they lived in the same city, their paths would never cross, because their two lives were worlds apart. He would never know what it was like to possess her. To feel those creamy curves beneath his fingers and her soft flesh parting as he thrust deep inside. He would never know what sound she made when she gasped out her orgasm, nor the powerful pleasure of spurting his seed deep inside her. She might be the wrong type of woman for him on so many levels— but not, he suspected, in bed.

Still mesmerised by the sway of her bottom, he began to follow her across the dance-floor, catching up with her by one of the bars, where she was refusing a cocktail.

She barely gave him a glance as he walked up beside her.

'You're not leaving?' he said.

'I can't leave. At least, not until Michela has thrown her bouquet and driven off into the night with Lucas. But after that, you won't see me for dust, I promise.'

'Before you make any promises—I have a proposition you might like to hear.'

'I don't need to hear it,' she said flatly. 'I wouldn't need to be a genius to work out what you might have in mind, after the things you said on the dance-floor and the way you were holding me. And it doesn't make any difference.' She sucked in a deep breath and met his gaze. 'I'm not interested in having sex with you, Niccolò—got that?'

Niccolò wondered if she knew how blatantly her nipples were contradicting her words—but maybe now wasn't the time to tell her.

'But what if it was a business proposition?' he questioned.

Her eyes narrowed. 'What kind of business proposition?'

He looked at the waxy white flowers which were woven into her hair and he wanted to reach out and crush them between his fingers. He wanted to press his lips on hers. He wanted to undress her and feast his eyes on that soft, creamy body. In a world where he had managed to achieve every single one of his objectives, he suddenly recognised that Alannah Collins had been a residual thorn in his flesh. A faint but lingering memory of a pleasure which had eluded him.

But not for much longer.

He smiled. 'You said you were an interior designer and suggested I have a look at your website, which I did. And you *are* good. In fact, you are very good. Which means that you have a skill and I have a need,' he said.

Her mouth thinned into a prudish line. 'I don't think that your needs are the kind I necessarily cater for.'

'I think we're talking at cross purposes, Alannah. This has nothing to do with sex.' He slanted her a thoughtful look. 'Does the name Park View ring any bells?'

'You mean that enormous new apartment block overlooking Hyde Park which has been disrupting the Knightsbridge traffic for months?'

'That's the one.'

'What about it?'

'It's mine. I own it. I built it.'

Alannah blinked. 'But it's the most...'

'Don't be shy, Alannah,' he said softly as her voice tailed off. 'One should never be shy when talking about money. It's the most expensive building of its kind in the world—isn't that what you were going to say?'

She shrugged. 'I fail to see how your property port-folio could possibly interest me.'

'Then hear me out. A friend of mine—a brilliant Greek named Alekto Sarantos—is about to complete one of the penthouse apartments.'

She lifted her hand to adjust a stray petal on her headdress. 'And is there a problem?'

'*Sì.* Or at least—he certainly seems to think there is.' A note of irritation entered his voice. 'The prob-lem is that Alekto doesn't like the décor, even though it has been overseen by one of the most popular de-signers in the city.'

'Let me guess.' She raised her eyebrows. 'Cream walls? Bowls of big pebbles lying around the place? Lots of glass and neutral-coloured blinds?'

He frowned. 'You must have seen photos.'

'I don't need to, but I'd recognise a bandwagon

anywhere—and every interior designer in the business seems to be jumping on it. Presumably this friend of yours doesn't do bland and that's why he doesn't like it.'

'No, Alekto doesn't do bland—in fact, he is the antithesis of bland. He described the décor to my assistant as a "tsunami of beige" and unless I can transform the place to his satisfaction before the Greek new year, then he says he'll pull out of the deal and go to Paris instead. It has become a matter of pride for me that he chooses London.' He gave a hard smile. 'And maybe that's where you could come in.'

'Me?'

'You want a break, don't you? I don't imagine they get much bigger than this.'

'But...' Somehow she managed to keep the tremble of excitement from her voice. 'Why me? There must be a million other designers itching to accept a job like this.'

His gaze swept over her like an icy black searchlight—objective, speculative and entirely without emotion.

'Because I like your style,' he said unexpectedly. 'I like the way you dress and the way you look. I always have. And if you can satisfy my exacting friend with your designs—then the job is yours.'

Alannah felt ridiculously thrilled by his praise, yet she didn't want to be thrilled. She wanted to feel nothing. To give nothing and take nothing. She met his dark gaze. 'And the fact that you want to go to bed with me has nothing to do with your offer, I suppose?'

He gave a soft laugh. 'Oh, but it has everything to do with it, *mia sirena*,' he said. 'As you said yourself, there are a million interior designers out there, but your desirability gives you a distinctive edge over your competitors. I cannot deny that I want you or that I intend to have you.' His black eyes gleamed. 'But I wouldn't dream of offering you the job unless I thought you were capable of delivering.'

CHAPTER FOUR

'NICCOLÒ WILL SEE you in just a moment, Alannah.'
The redhead sitting outside Niccolò's office wore a
silk blouse the colour of the lilies on her desk and
when she smiled her lips were a neat coral curve. 'My
name's Kirsty, by the way—and I'm one of Niccolò's
assistants. Take a seat over there. Can I get you a coffee? Some tea perhaps?'

'No. I'm fine, thanks.' Carefully putting down her
mood-boards, Alannah sank onto a seat, wondering if
any of her reservations showed in her face. Whether
her nerves or sick dread were visible to the impar-
tial observer.

Ever since she'd left New York, she had listed all
the reasons why she should say no to Niccolò's offer of
work and during the cramped flight she had checked
them off on her fingers. He was arrogant. Tick. He
was dangerous. Double tick. He was also completely
unapologetic about wanting to take her to bed. Only
he hadn't even said *that* in a flattering way. He'd made
it sound as if she was just something he needed to
get out of his system. Like an itch. Or a fever. She bit
her lip because his attitude brought too many memories flooding back. She hated men who regarded a

woman as some kind of *object*, so surely self-respect and pride should have made her turn his offer down, no matter how lucrative?

But he was offering her work—legitimate work. His proposition had been like a cool drink when your throat was parched. Like finding a crumpled ten-pound note in your jeans before you washed them. She thought about the scarcity of jobs in her highly competitive field, and the ridiculously high mortgage on her tiny bedsit. She couldn't *afford* to turn him down—which was why she'd spent all weekend coming up with ideas she thought might appeal to a Greek billionaire who didn't like beige. And through it all she had realised that this was the vital springboard her career needed and she was going to grab at it with both hands.

She stared at the cream lilies on Kirsty's desk, trying to concentrate on their stark beauty, but all she could think about was the way Niccolò had stroked his finger over her when they'd been dancing at the wedding. Her heart began to pound. It had been an almost *innocent* touch and yet her response had been anything but innocent. The intensity of her feelings had shocked her. She had wanted him to peel the bridesmaid dress from her body and touch her properly. She had wanted him to kiss her the way he'd done all those years before—only this time not to stop.

And that was the problem.

She still wanted him.

She had done her best to quash that thought when she'd emailed him some suggestions. And had attempted to ignore her spiralling feeling of excitement when his reply came winging into her inbox late last night.

These are good. Be at my offices tomorrow at 7p.m.

It hadn't been the most fulsome praise she'd ever received, but it was clear he considered her good enough for the job and that pleased her more than it should have done. And hot on the heels of professional pride came a rather more unexpected feeling of gratitude. She had stared at his email and realised that, no matter what his motives might be, Niccolò was giving her the chance to make something of herself.

So she'd better show him that his faith had not been misplaced.

A buzzer sounded on Kirsty's desk and she rose to her feet, opening a set of double doors directly behind her.

'Niccolò is ready for you now, Alannah.' She smiled. 'If you'd like to come this way.'

Alannah picked up her mood-boards and followed Kirsty into a huge and airy office, blinking a little as she looked around her, because she'd never been anywhere like this before. She gulped. It was...*spectacular.* One wall consisted entirely of glass and overlooked some of London's more familiar landmarks and Alannah was so dazzled by the view that it took a moment for her to notice Niccolò sitting there and to realise that he wasn't alone.

Her first thought was how at home he looked in the luxury of his palatial surroundings. Long legs stretched out in front of him, he was reclining on a large leather sofa in one corner of the vast office—and opposite him was a man with black hair and the bluest eyes she'd ever seen. This must be Alekto Sarantos, Alannah thought, but she barely noticed him. Despite his unmistakable gorgeousness, it was Niccolò who captured her attention. Niccolò whose outwardly relaxed stance couldn't quite disguise the tension in his powerful body as their gazes clashed and held. She could read the mockery in his eyes. *I know how much you want me,* they seemed to say. And suddenly she wished that the floor could swallow her up or that the nerves which were building up inside her would show her some mercy and leave her alone.

'Ah, Alannah. Here you are.' Black eyes glittered with faint amusement as he looked her up and down. 'Not jet-lagged, I hope?'

'Not at all,' she lied politely.

'Let me introduce you to Alekto Sarantos. Alekto—this is Alannah Collins, the very talented designer I was telling you about.'

Alannah gave an uncertain smile, wondering exactly *what* he'd said about her. They were friends, weren't they? And didn't men boast to their mates about what they'd done with a woman? She could feel her cheeks growing slightly warm as she looked at Alekto. 'I'm very pleased to meet you.'

'Do sit down,' he said, in a gravelly Greek accent.

Alannah saw Niccolò pat the space beside him on the sofa—and she thought it looked a bit like someone encouraging a dog to leap up. But she forced herself to smile as she sat down next to him, unwinding the vivid green pashmina which was looped around her neck.

Alekto turned his startling blue gaze on her. 'So...

Niccolò assures me that you are the person who can replace the existing décor with something a little more imaginative.' He grimaced. 'Although frankly, a piece of wood could have produced something more eye-catching than the existing scheme.'

'I'm confident I can, Mr Sarantos.'

'No. *Parakalo*—you must call me Alekto,' he said, a hint of impatience hardening his voice, before giving a swift smile. 'I always like to hear a beautiful woman saying my name.'

Beautiful? No woman ever thought she was beautiful and that certainly hadn't been the effect Alannah had been striving for today. She'd aimed for a functional, rather than a decorative appearance—tying her hair back in a thick plait to stop it being whipped up by the fierce December wind. She had wanted to project style and taste as well as hoping her clothes would be like armour—protecting her from Niccolò's heated gaze.

Her Japanese-inspired grey dress bore the high neckline which had become her trademark and the fitted waist provided structure. A glittering scarab beetle brooch and funky ankle-boots added the unconventional twists which she knew were necessary to transform the ordinary into something different. It was the detail which counted. Everyone knew that.

'If you insist,' she said, with another polite smile. 'Alekto.'

Niccolò raised his eyebrows. 'Perhaps you'd like to show *Alekto* what ideas you have in mind for his apartment, while he concentrates on your undoubted beauty,' he suggested drily.

Trying to ignore the sarcasm in his voice, Alannah

spread out the mood-boards she'd been working on and watched as Alekto began to study them. Squares of contemporary brocade were pasted next to splashes of paint colour, and different swatches of velvet and silk added to the textural diversity she had in mind.

'We could go either traditional or contemporary,' she said. 'But I definitely think you need something a little bolder in terms of colour. The walls would work well in greeny-greys and muted blues—which would provide a perfect backdrop for these fabrics and textiles and reflect your love of the sea.'

'Did Niccolò tell you that I love the sea?' questioned Alekto idly.

'No. I searched your name on the Internet and had a look at your various homes around the world. You do seem rather fond of sea views and that gave me a few ideas.'

'Enterprising,' Alekto commented, flicking through each page, before lifting his head. *'Neh.* This is perfect. All of it. You have chosen well, Niccolò. This is a huge improvement. You have pleased me, Alannah—and a woman who pleases a man should always be rewarded. I think I shall take you out for dinner tonight, to thank you.'

'I'm sure Alannah would love nothing more,' interjected Niccolò smoothly, 'but, unfortunately, she is already committed this evening.'

'Really?' Alekto raised dark and imperious brows. 'I'm sure she could cancel whatever it is she is *committed* to.'

'Possibly.' Niccolò shrugged. 'But only if you are prepared to wait for your apartment to be completed, my friend. Time is of the essence if you expect it to be ready for your new year party. Isn't that what you wanted?'

The gazes of the two men clashed and Alekto's eyes suddenly hardened with comprehension.

'Ah,' he said softly as he rose to his feet. 'Suddenly, I begin to understand. You have always been a great connoisseur of beauty, Niccolò. And since good friends do not poach, I shall leave you in peace.' His blue eyes glittered. 'Enjoy.'

Alekto's chauvinistic innuendo took Alannah by surprise but she reminded herself that she was simply working for him—she wasn't planning on having him as her friend. Keeping her lips clamped into a tight smile, she stood up to let him shake her hand, before Niccolò led him into the outer office.

She waited until the Sicilian had returned and closed the door behind him before she turned on him.

'What was that all about?' she questioned quietly.

'What?' He walked over to his desk, stabbing at a button on his telephone pad, so that a red light appeared. 'The fact that your designs pleased him? Alekto is one of the wealthiest men I know. You should be delighted. The patronage of a man like that is more priceless than rubies.' He looked at her, his eyes curiously flat and assessing. 'Who knows what kind of opportunities could now come your way, Alannah. Especially since he clearly finds you so attractive.'

'No, none of that!' She shook her head—hating the way he was looking at her. Hating the way he was talking about her. 'I don't care that he's rich—other than it means I will have a very generous budget to work with. And I don't care whether or not he finds me attractive. I'd like it if for once we could keep my looks out of it, since I'm supposed to be here on merit.' She stared at him. 'What I'm talking about is you telling him I was busy and couldn't have dinner with him tonight.'

'Did you want to have dinner with him?'

'That's beside the point.'

He slanted her a look. 'I'm not sure what your point is.'

'That I don't want you or anyone else answering for me because I like to make my own decisions. And...' she hesitated '...you have no right to be territorial about me.'

'No,' he said slowly. 'I realise that.'

She narrowed her eyes warily. 'You mean you're agreeing with me?'

He shrugged. 'For a man to behave in a territorial way towards a woman implies that she is his. That she has given herself to him in some way. And you haven't, have you, Alannah?' The eyes which a moment ago had looked so flat now gleamed like polished jet. 'Of course, that is something which could be changed in a heartbeat. We both know that.'

Alannah stiffened as his gaze travelled over her and she could feel her throat growing dry. And wasn't it crazy that, no matter how much her mind protested, she couldn't seem to stop her body from responding to his lazy scrutiny. She found herself thinking how easy it would be to go along with his suggestion. To surrender to the ache deep inside her and have him take all her frustration away. All she had to do was smile—a quick, complicit smile—and that would be the only green light he needed.

And then what?

She swallowed. A mindless coupling with someone who'd made no secret of his contempt for her? An act which would inevitably leave him triumphant and her, what? *Empty*, that was what.

A lifetime of turning down sexual invitations meant that she knew exactly how to produce the kind of brisk smile which would destabilise the situation without causing a scene. But for once, it took a real effort.

'I think not,' she said, scooping up her pashmina from the sofa. 'I have a self-protective instinct which warns me off intimacy with a certain kind of man, and I'm afraid you're one of them. The things I require from you are purely practical, Niccolò. I need a list of craftsmen—painters and decorators—who you use on your properties and who I assume will be available to work for me—and to work very quickly if we're to get this job in on time.'

The impatient wave of his hand told her that painters and decorators were of no interest to him. 'Speak to Kirsty about it.'

'I will.' She hitched the strap of her bag further over her shoulder. 'And if that's everything—I'll get going.'

He nodded. 'I'll drive you home.'

'That won't be necessary.'

'You have your own car?'

Was he kidding? Didn't he realise that car parking costs in London put motoring way beyond the reach of mere mortals? Alannah shook her head. 'I always use public transport.'

'Then I will take you. I insist.' His eyes met hers

with cool challenge. 'Unless you'd prefer to travel by train on a freezing December night, rather than in the warm comfort of my car?'

'You're boxing me into a corner, Niccolò.'

'I know I am. But you'll find it's a very comfortable box.' He took his car keys from his jacket pocket. 'Come.'

In the elevator, she kept her distance. Just as she kept her gaze trained on the flashing arrow as it took them down to the underground car park, where his car was waiting.

He punched her postcode into his satnav and didn't say another word as they drove along the busy streets of Knightsbridge, where Christmas shoppers were crowding the frosty pavements. Alannah peered out of the window. Everywhere was bright with coloured lights and gifts and people looking at the seasonal displays in Harrods's windows.

The car turned into Trafalgar Square and the famous Christmas tree loomed into view and suddenly Alannah felt the painful twist of her heart. It was funny how grief hit you when you least expected it—in a fierce wave which made your eyes grow all wet and salty. She remembered coming here with her mother, when they were waiting for the result of her biopsy. When standing looking up at a giant tree on an icy winter night had seemed like the perfect city outing. There'd been hardly any money in their purses, but they'd still had hope. Until a half-hour session with a man in a white coat had quashed that hope and they'd never been able to get it back again.

She blinked away the tears as the car began to speed towards West London, hoping that Niccolò's concentration on the traffic meant he hadn't noticed. He reached out to put some music on—something Italian and passionate, which filled the air and made her heart clench again, but this time with a mixture of pleasure and pain.

Closing her eyes, she let the powerful notes wash over her and when she opened them again the landscape had altered dramatically. The houses in this part of the city were much closer together and as Niccolò turned off the main road a few stray traces of garbage fluttered like ghosts along the pavement.

'Is this where you live?' he questioned.

She heard the faint incredulity in his voice and realised that this was exactly why she hadn't wanted this lift. *Because he will judge you. He will judge you and find you wanting, just as he's always done.* 'That's right,' she said.

He killed the engine and turned to look at her, his dark features brooding in the shadowed light.

'It's not what I expected.'

Her question was light, almost coquettish. She wondered if he could tell she'd been practising saying it in her head. 'And what *did* you expect?'

For a moment Niccolò didn't answer, because once again she had confounded his expectations. He had imagined a pricey location—a fortified mansion flat bought on the proceeds of the money she'd earned from *Stacked* magazine. Or a cute little mews cottage in Holland Park. Somewhere brimming with the kind of wealthy men who might enjoy dabbling with a woman as beautiful as her.

But *this*...

The unmistakable signs of poverty were all around

them. The rubbish on the pavement. A battered car with its wing-mirror missing. The shadowy group of youths in their hoodies, who stood watching their car with silent menace.

'What happened to all your money?' he questioned suddenly. 'You must have earned—'

'Stacks?' she questioned pointedly.

His smile was brief as he acknowledged the pun. 'A lot.'

She stared down at her handbag. 'It was a short-lived career—it didn't exactly provide me with a gold-plated pension.'

'So what did you do with it?'

I paid for my mother's medical bills. I chased a miracle which was never going to happen. I chased it until the pot was almost empty though the outcome hadn't changed one bit. She shrugged, tempted to tell him that it was none of his business—but she sensed that here was a man who wouldn't give up. Who would dig away until he had extracted everything he needed to know. She tried to keep her words light and flippant, but suddenly it wasn't easy. 'Oh, I frittered it all away. As you do.'

Niccolò looked at the unexpected tremble of her lips and frowned, because that sudden streak of vulnerability she was trying so hard to disguise was completely unexpected. Was she regretting the money she had squandered? Did she lay awake at night and wonder how the hell she had ended up in a place like this? He tried and failed to imagine how she fitted in here. Despite all her attempts to subdue her innate sensuality and tame her voluptuous appearance, she must still stand out like a lily tossed carelessly into a muddy gutter.

And suddenly he wanted to kiss her. The street-light was casting an unworldly orange light over her creamy skin, so that she looked like a ripe peach just begging to be eaten. He felt temptation swelling up inside him, like a slow and insistent storm. Almost without thinking, he found himself reaching out to touch her cheek, wondering if it felt as velvety-soft as it appeared. And it did. Oh, God, it did. A whisper of longing licked over his skin.

'What...what do you think you're doing?' she whispered.

'You know damned well what I'm doing,' he said unsteadily. 'I'm giving into something which has always been there and which is refusing to die. Something which gets stronger each time we see each another. So why don't we just give into it, Alannah— and see where it takes us?'

She knew it was coming. Of course she did. She'd been kissed by enough men to recognise the sudden roughening of his voice and opaque smoulder of his black eyes. But no man had ever kissed her the way Niccolò did.

Time slowed as he bent his face towards hers and she realised he was giving her enough time to stop him. But she didn't. How could she when she wanted this so much? She just let him anchor her with the masterful slide of his hands as they captured the back of her head, before he crushed his lips down on hers.

Instantly, she moaned. It was ten long years since he'd kissed her and already she was on fire. She felt *consumed* by it. Powered by it. Need washed over her as she splayed her palms against his chest as his tongue licked its way into her mouth—her lips opened greedily, as if urging him to go deeper. She heard his responding murmur, as if her eagerness pleased him, and something made her bunch her hands into fists and drum them against his torso—resenting and wanting him all at the same time.

He raised his head, dark eyes burning into her like fire. But there were no subtle nuances to his voice now—just a mocking question in an accent which suddenly sounded harsh and *very* Sicilian. 'Are you trying to hurt me, *bella*?'

'I—yes! *Yes!*' She wanted to hurt him first—before he had the chance to do it to her.

He gave a soft laugh—as if recognising his own power and exulting in it. 'But I am not going to let you,' he said softly. 'We are going to give each other pleasure, not pain.'

Alannah's head tipped back as he reached down to cup her breast through the heavy silk of her dress. And she let him. Actually, she did more than let him. Her breathless sighs encouraged him to go even further, and he did.

He kissed her neck as his hand crept down to alight on one stockinged knee. And wasn't it shameful that she had parted her knees—praying he would move his hand higher to where the ache was growing unbearable? But he didn't—at least, not at first. For a while he seemed content to tease her. To bring her to such a pitch of excitement that she squirmed with impatience—wriggling restlessly until at last he moved his hand to skate it lightly over her thigh. She heard him suck in a breath of approval as he encountered the bare skin above her stocking top and she shivered as she felt his fingers curl possessively over the goose-pimpled flesh.

'I am pleased to see that despite the rather staid outfits you seem to favour, you still dress to tantalise underneath,' he said. 'And I need to undress you very quickly, before I go out of my mind with longing. I need to see that beautiful body for myself.'

His words killed it. Just like that. They shattered the spell he'd woven and wiped out all the desire—replacing it with a dawning horror of what she'd almost allowed to happen.

Allowed?

Who was she kidding? She might as well have presented herself to him in glittery paper all tied up with a gift ribbon. He'd given her a lift home and just assumed...*assumed*...

He'd assumed he could start treating her like a pin-up instead of a person. Somewhere along the way she had stopped being Alannah and had become a body he simply wanted to ogle. Why had she thought he was different from every other man?

'What am I doing?' she demanded, jerking away from him and lifting her fingertips to her lips in horror. 'What am I *thinking* of?'

'Oh, come on, Alannah.' He began to tap his finger impatiently against the steering wheel. 'We're both a little too *seasoned* to play this kind of game, surely? You might *just* have got away with the outraged virgin scenario a decade ago, but not any more. I'm pretty sure your track record must be almost as extensive as mine. So why the sudden shutdown at exactly the wrong moment, when we both know we want it?'

It took everything she had for Alannah not to fly at him until she remembered that, in spite of everything, he was still her boss. She realised she couldn't keep blaming him for leaping to such unflattering conclusions, because why *wouldn't* he think she'd been around the block several times? Nice girls didn't take off their clothes for the camera, did they? And nice girls didn't part their legs for a man who didn't respect them.

'You might have a reputation as one of the world's greatest lovers, Niccolò,' she said, 'but right now, it's difficult to see why.'

She saw his brows knit together as he glowered at her. 'What are you talking about?'

Grabbing the handle, she pushed open the car door and a blast of cold air came rushing inside, mercifully cooling her heated face. 'Making out in the front of cars is what teenagers do,' she bit out. 'I thought you had a little bit more finesse than that. Most men at least offer dinner.'

CHAPTER FIVE

EVERY TIME NICCOLÒ closed his eyes he could imagine those lips lingering on a certain part of his anatomy. He could picture it with a clarity which was like a prolonged and exquisite torture. He gave a groan of frustration and slammed his fist into the pillow. Was Alannah Collins aware that she was driving him crazy with need?

Turning onto his back, he stared up at the ceiling. Of course she was. Her *profession*—if you could call it that—had been pandering to male fantasy. She must have learnt that men were turned on by stockings— and socks. By tousled hair and little-girl pouts. By big blue eyes and beautiful breasts.

Had she subsequently learnt as she'd grown older that teasing and concealment could be almost as much of a turn-on? That to a man used to having everything he wanted, even the *idea* of a woman refusing sex was enough to make his body burn with a hunger which was pretty close to unbearable. Did she often let men caress the bare and silky skin of her thigh and then push them away just when they were in tantalising reach of far more intimate contact?

Frustratedly running his fingers through his hair, he got out of bed and headed for the bathroom.

If she hadn't been such a damned hypocrite when she'd slammed her way out of his car last night, then he wouldn't be feeling this way. If she'd been honest enough to admit what she really wanted, he wouldn't have woken up feeling aching and empty. She could have invited him in and turned those denim-blue eyes on him and let nature take its course. They could have spent the night together and he would have got her out of his system, once and for all.

He turned on the shower, welcoming the icy water which lashed over his heated skin.

True, her home hadn't looked particularly *inviting*. It didn't look big enough to accommodate much more than a single bed, let alone any degree of comfort. But that was okay. His mouth hardened. Mightn't the sheer *ordinariness* of the environment have added a piquant layer of excitement to a situation he resented himself for wanting?

Agitatedly, he rubbed shampoo into his hair, thinking that she made him want to break every rule in the book and he didn't like it. The women he dated were chosen as carefully as his suits and he didn't do *bad girls*. His taste tended towards corporate bankers. Or lawyers. He liked them blonde and he liked them cool. He liked the kind of woman who never sweated...

Not like Alannah Collins. He swallowed as the water sluiced down over his heated skin. He could imagine *her* sweating. He closed his eyes and imagined her riding him—her long black hair damp with exertion as it swung around her luscious breasts. He turned off the shower, trying to convince himself that the experience would be fleeting and shallow. It would be like eating fast food after you'd been on a health kick. The first greasy mouthful would taste like heaven but by the time you'd eaten the last crumb, you'd be longing for something pure and simple.

So why not forget her?

He got ready for the office and spent the rest of the week trying to do just that. He didn't go near Alekto's apartment, just listened to daily progress reports from Kirsty. He kept himself busy, successfully bidding for a new-build a few blocks from the Pembroke in New York. He held a series of back-to-back meetings about his beach development in Uruguay; he lunched with a group of developers who were over from the Middle East—then took them to a nightclub until the early hours. Then he flew to Paris and had dinner with a beautiful Australian model he'd met at last year's Melbourne Cup.

But Paris didn't work and neither did the model. For once the magic of the city failed to cast its spell on him. Overnight it had surrendered to the monster which was Christmas and spread its glittering tentacles everywhere. The golden lights which were strung in the trees along the Champs Élysées seemed garish. The decorated tree in his hotel seemed like a giant monument to bad taste and the pile of faux-presents which rested at its base made his mouth harden with disdain. Even the famous shops were stuffed with seasonal reminders of reindeer and Santa, which marred their usual elegance.

And all this was underpinned by the disturbing fact that nothing was working; he couldn't seem to get Alannah out of his mind. *Even now.* He realised that something about her was making him act out of character. There were plenty of other people whose style he liked, yet he had hired her without reference and only the most cursory of glances at her work. Governed by a need to possess her, he had ignored all reason and common sense and done something he'd sworn never to do.

He had taken a gamble on her.

He felt the icy finger of fear whispering over his spine.

He had taken a gamble on her and he never gambled.

He ordered his driver to take him to the towering block which rose up over Hyde Park. But for once he didn't take pride in the futuristic building which had been his brainchild, and which had won all kinds of awards since its inception. All he could think about was the slow build of hunger which was burning away inside him and which was now refusing to be silenced.

His heart was thudding as he took the elevator up to the penthouse, his key-card quietly clicking the door open. Silently, he walked through the bare apartment, which smelt strongly of paint, and into the main reception room where he found Alannah perched on a stepladder, a tape measure in her hand.

His heart skipped a beat. She wore a loose, checked shirt and her hair was caught back in a ponytail. He didn't know what he'd been planning to say but before he had a chance to say anything she turned round and saw him. The stepladder swayed and he walked across the room to steady it and some insane part of him wished it would topple properly, so that he could catch her in his arms and feel the soft crush of her breasts against him.

'N-Niccolò,' she said, her fingers curling around one of the ladder's rungs.

'Me,' he agreed.

She licked her lips. 'I wasn't expecting you.'

'Should I have rung to make an appointment?'

'Of...of course not,' she said stiffly. 'What can I do for you?'

His eyes narrowed. She was acting as if they were strangers—like two people who'd met briefly at a party. Had she forgotten the last time he'd seen her, when their mouths had been hot and hungry and they'd been itching to get inside each other's clothes? Judging from the look on her face, it might as well have been a figment of his imagination. He forced himself to look around the room—as if he were remotely interested in what she was doing with it. 'I thought I'd better see how work is progressing.'

'Yes, of course.' She began to clamber down the ladder, stuffing the tape measure into the pocket of her jeans. 'I know it doesn't look like very much at the moment, but it will all come together when everything's in place. That...' Her finger was shaking a little as she pointed. 'That charcoal shade is a perfect backdrop for some of the paintings which Alekto is having shipped over from Greece.'

'Good. What else?' He began to walk through the apartment and she followed him, her canvas shoes squeaking a little on the polished wooden floors.

'Here, in the study, I've used Aegean Almond as a colour base,' she said. 'I thought it was kind of appropriate.'

'Aegean Almond?' he echoed. 'What kind of lunatic comes up with a name like that?'

'You'd better not go into the bathroom, then,' she warned, her lips twitching. 'Because you'll find Cigarette Smoke everywhere.'

'There's really a paint called Cigarette Smoke?'

'I'm afraid there is.'

He started to laugh and Alannah found herself joining in, before hurriedly clamping her mouth shut. Because humour was dangerous and just because he'd been amused by something she'd said it didn't mean he'd suddenly undergone a personality transplant. He had an *agenda*. A selfish agenda, which didn't take any of *her* wishes into account and that was because he was a selfish man. Niccolò got what Niccolò wanted and it was vital she didn't allow herself to be added to his long list of acquisitions.

She realised he was still looking at her.

'So everything's running according to schedule?' he said.

She nodded. 'I've ordered velvet sofas and sourced lamps and smaller pieces of furniture.'

'Good.'

Was that enough? she wondered. How much detail did he need to know to be convinced she was doing a good job? Because no matter what he thought about her past, he needed to know she wasn't going to let him down. She cleared her throat. 'And I've picked up some gorgeous stuff on the King's Road.'

'You've obviously got everything under control.'

'I hope so. That is what you're paying me for.'

Niccolò walked over to the window and stared out at the uninterrupted view of Hyde Park. The wintry trees were bare and the pewter sky seemed heavy with the threat of snow. It seemed as if his hunch about her ability had been right. It seemed she was talented, as well as beautiful.

And suddenly he realised he couldn't keep taking his anger out on her. Who *cared* what kind of life she'd led? Who cared about anything except possessing her? Composing his face into the kind of expression which was usually guaranteed to get him exactly what he wanted, Niccolò smiled.

'It looks perfect,' he said. 'You must let me buy you dinner.'

She shook her head. 'Honestly, you don't have to do that.'

'No?' He raised his eyebrows in mocking question. 'The other night you seemed to imply you felt short-changed because I'd made a pass at you without jumping through the necessary social hoops first.'

'That was different.'

'How?'

She lifted her hand to fiddle unnecessarily with her ponytail. 'I made the comment in response to a situation.'

'A situation which won't seem to go away.' His black eyes lanced into her. 'Unless something has changed and you're going to deny that you want me?'

She sighed. 'I don't think I'm a good enough actress to do that, Niccolò. But wanting you doesn't automatically mean that I'm going to do anything about it. You must have women wanting you every day of the week.'

'But we're not talking about other women. What if I just wanted the opportunity to redeem myself?

To show you that I am really just a…what is it you say?' He lifted his shoulders and his hands in an exaggerated gesture of incomprehension. 'Ah, yes. A regular guy.'

'Of course you are.' She laughed, in spite of herself. 'Describing you as a regular guy would be like calling a thirty-carat diamond a trinket.'

'Oh, come on, Alannah,' he urged softly. 'One dinner between a boss and his employee. What's the harm in that?'

Alannah could think of at least ten answers, but the trouble was that when he asked her like that, with those black eyes blazing into her, all her reservations slipped right out of her mind. Which was how she found herself in the back of a big black limousine later that evening, heading for central London. She was sitting as far away from Niccolò as possible but even so—her palms were still clammy with nerves and her heart racing with excitement.

'So where are we going?' she questioned, looking at the burly set of the driver's shoulders through the tinted glass screen which divided them.

'The Vinoly,' Niccolò said. 'Do you know it?'

She shook her head. She'd heard about it, of course. Currently London's most fashionable venue, it was famous for being impossible to get a table though Niccolò was greeted with the kind of delight which suggested that he might be a regular.

The affluence of the place was undeniable. The women wore designer and diamonds while the men seemed to have at least three mobile phones lined up neatly beside their bread plates and their gazes kept straying to them.

Alannah told herself she wasn't going to be intimidated even though she still couldn't quite believe she'd agreed to come. As she'd got ready she had tried to convince herself that exposure to Niccolò's arrogance might be enough to kill her desire for him, once and for all.

But the reality was turning out to be nothing like she'd imagined. Why hadn't she taken into account his charisma—or at least prepared herself for a great onslaught of it? Because suddenly there seemed nothing in her armoury to help her withstand it.

She had never been with a man who commanded quite so much attention. She saw the pianist nodding to him, with a smile. She saw other diners casting surreptitious glances at him, even though they were pretending not to. But it was more than his obvious wealth which drew people's gaze, like a magnet. Beneath the sophisticated exterior, he radiated a raw masculinity which radiated from his powerful body like a dark aura.

They sat down at a discreet table but suddenly the complex menu seemed too rich for a stomach which was sick with nerves. Alannah found herself wishing she were eating an omelette at her own kitchen table rather than subjecting herself to a maelstrom of emotions which were making her feel most peculiar.

'What are you going to have?' asked Niccolò as the waiter appeared.

The words on the menu had blurred into incomprehensible lines and she lifted her gaze to him. 'I don't know. You order for me,' she said recklessly.

He raised his eyebrows before giving their order but once the waiter had gone he turned to study her, his black eyes thoughtful. 'Are you usually quite so accommodating?'

'Not usually, no.' She smoothed her napkin. 'But then, this isn't what you'd call *usual*, is it?'

'In what way?'

'Well.' She shrugged. 'You made it sound like a working dinner, but it feels a bit like a date.'

'And what if we pretended it was a date—would that help you relax a little more?'

'To be honest, it's been so long since I've been on a date that I've almost forgotten what it's like,' she said slowly.

He took a sip of water which didn't quite disguise the sudden cynicism of his smile. 'I find that very difficult to believe.'

She laughed. 'I'm sure you do—given your apparent love of stereotypes. What's the matter, Niccolò—doesn't that fit in with your image of me? You think that because I once took off my clothes for the camera, that I have men queuing up outside the bedroom door?'

'Do you?'

'Not half as many as you, I bet,' she said drily.

They were staring at one another across the table, their eyes locked in silent battle, when suddenly he leaned towards her, his words so low that only she could hear them.

'Why did you do it, Alannah?' he questioned roughly. 'Wasn't it bad enough that you were kicked out of school for smoking dope and playing truant? Why the hell did you cheapen yourself by stripping off?'

The waiter chose precisely that moment to light the

small candle at the centre of the table. And that short gap provided Alannah with enough time for rebellion to flare into life inside her.

'Why do you think I did it?' she demanded. 'Why do people usually do jobs like that? Because I needed the money.'

'For what?' His lips curled. 'To end up in a poky apartment in one of the tougher ends of town?'

'Oh, you're so quick to judge, aren't you, Niccolò? So eager to take the moral high ground, when you don't have a clue what was going on in my life and you never did! Did you know that when my mother handed in her notice, she never found another job to match that one—probably because the reference the school gave her was so grudging. Did you know that they got all their clever lawyers to pick over her contract and that she lost all her rights?'

His eyes narrowed. 'What kind of rights?'

'There was no pension provision made for her and the salary she got in lieu of notice was soon swallowed up by the cost of settling back in England. She couldn't find another live-in job, so she became an agency nurse—with no fixed contract. I had to go to a local sixth-form college to take my exams and at first, I hated it. But we were just beginning to pick ourselves up again when...'

Her voice tailed off and his words broke into the silence.

'What happened?' he demanded.

She shook her head. 'It doesn't matter.'

'It *does*.'

Alannah hesitated, not wanting to appear vulnerable—because vulnerability made you weak. But wasn't anything better than having him look at her with that look of utter *condemnation* on his face? Shouldn't Niccolò da Conti learn that it was wise to discover all the facts before you condemned someone outright?

'She got cancer,' she said baldly. 'She'd actually had it for quite a long time but she'd been ignoring the symptoms so she didn't have to take any unnecessary time off work. By the time she went to see the doctor, the disease was advanced and she was scared,' she said, swallowing down the sudden lump in her throat. They'd both been scared. 'There was nobody but me and her. She was only a relatively young woman and she didn't want...' The lump seemed to have grown bigger. 'She didn't want to die.'

'Alannah—'

But she shook her head, because she didn't want his sympathy. She didn't *need* his sympathy.

'Our doctor told us about an experimental drug trial which was being done in the States,' she said. 'And early indications were that the treatment was looking hopeful, but it was prohibitively expensive and impossible to get funding for it.'

And suddenly Niccolò understood. Against the snowy tablecloth, he clenched his hands into tight fists. *'Bedda matri!'* he said raggedly. 'You did those photos to pay for your mother to go to America?'

'Bravo,' she said shakily. 'Now do you see? It gave me power—the power to help her. The thought of all that money was beyond my wildest dreams and there was no way I could have turned it down.' *No matter how many men had leered in her face afterwards. No matter that people like Niccolò judged her*

*and looked down their noses at her or thought that
she'd be up for easy sex because of it.* 'My unique
selling point was that I'd left one of the most exclusive Swiss finishing schools under rather ignomini-
ous circumstances and I guess I can't blame them
for wanting to capitalise on that. They told me that
plenty of men were turned on by girls in school uniform, and they were right. That's why that issue became their best-seller.'

Alarmed by the sudden whiteness of her face, he
pushed the wine glass towards her, but she shook her
head.

'It wasn't narcissism which motivated me, Niccolò—or a desire to flash my breasts like the exhibitionist you accused me of being. I did it because it's
the only way I could raise the money. I did it even
though I sometimes felt sick to the stomach with all
those men perving over me. But I hid my feelings
because I wanted to bring a miracle to my mother,
only the miracle never happened.' Her voice wavered
and it took a moment or two before she could steady
it enough to speak. 'She died the following spring.'

She did pick up her glass then, swilling down a
generous mouthful of red wine and choking a little.
But when she put the glass back down, she had to
lace her fingers together on the table-top, because she
couldn't seem to stop them from trembling.

'Alannah—'

'It's history,' she said, with a brisk shake of her
head. 'None of it matters now. I'm just telling you
what happened. I used the rest of the money to put
myself through art school and to put down a deposit
on a home. But property is expensive in London.

That's why I live where I do. That's why I chose to live in one of the "tougher" parts of London.'

Niccolò put his glass down with a hand which was uncharacteristically unsteady as a powerful wave of remorse washed over him. It was as if he was seeing her clearly for the first time—without the distortion of his own bigotry. He had judged her unfairly. He saw how she must have fought against the odds to free herself from a trap from which there had been no escaping. He'd fought against the odds himself, hadn't he? Though he realised now that his own choices had been far less stark than hers. And although he hated the solution she had chosen, he couldn't seem to stop himself from wanting to comfort her.

'I'm sorry,' he said huskily. 'For what happened and for the choices you had to make.'

She shrugged. 'Like I said, it's history.'

'Your mother was lucky to have a daughter like you, fighting for her like that,' he said suddenly. He found himself thinking that anyone would be glad to have her in their corner.

Her head was bent. 'Don't say any more,' she whispered. 'Please.'

He stared down at the plateful of cooling risotto which lay before him. 'Alannah?'

'What?'

Reluctantly, she lifted her head and he could see that her eyes were unnaturally bright. He thought how pale and wan she looked as he picked up his fork and scooped up some rice before guiding it towards her mouth. 'Open,' he instructed softly.

She shook her head. 'I'm not hungry.'

'Open,' he said again.

'Niccolò—'

'You need to eat something,' he said fiercely. 'Trust me. The food will make you feel better. Now eat the risotto.'

And although Alannah was reluctant, she was no match for his determination. She let him feed her that first forkful—all warm and buttery and fragrant with herbs—and then another. She felt some of the tension seep away from her, and then a little more. She ate in silence with his black eyes fixed on her and it felt like a curiously intimate thing for him to do, to feed her like that. Almost *tender*. Almost *protective*. And she needed to remember it was neither. It was just Niccolò appeasing his conscience. Maybe he'd finally realised that he'd been unnecessarily harsh towards her. This was probably just as much about repairing his image, as much as trying to brush over his own misjudgement.

And he was right about the food. Of course he was. It *did* make her feel much better. She could feel warmth creeping through her veins and the comforting flush of colour in her cheeks. She even smiled as he swopped plates and ate some himself while she sat back and watched him.

He dabbed at his lips with a napkin. 'Feel better now?'

'Yes.'

'But probably not in the mood to sit here and make small talk or to decide whether or not your waistline can cope with dessert?'

'You've got it in one,' she said.

'Then why don't I get the check, and we'll go?'

She'd assumed he would take her straight back to

Acton but once they were back in the car he made the driver wait. Outside, fairy lights twinkled in the two bay trees on either side of the restaurant door, but inside the car it was dark and shadowy. He turned to study her and all she could see was the gleam of his eyes as his gaze flickered over her face.

'I could take you home now,' he said. 'But I don't want the evening to end this way. It still feels...unfinished.'

'I'm not in the mood for a nightcap.'

'Neither am I.' He lifted his hand to her face and pushed back a thick strand of hair. 'I'm in the mood to touch you, but that seems unavoidable whenever you're near me.'

'Niccolò—'

'Don't,' he said unsteadily. 'Don't say a word.'

And stupidly, she didn't. She just sat there as he began to stroke her cheek and for some crazy reason she found that almost as reassuring as the way he'd fed her dinner. Was she so hungry for human comfort that she would take anything from a man she suspected could offer nothing but heartbreak?

'Niccolò—'

This time he silenced her protest with the touch of his lips against hers. A barely-there kiss which started her senses quivering. She realised that he was teasing her. Playing with her and tantalising her. And it was working. Oh, yes, it was working. She had to fight to keep her hands in her lap and not cling onto him like someone who'd found themselves a handy rock in a rough sea.

He drew away and looked into her face and Alannah realised that this was a Niccolò she'd never seen before. His face was grave, almost…assessing. She imagined this was how he might look in the board-room, before making a big decision.

'Now we could pretend that nothing's happening,' he said, as calmly as if he were discussing the markets. 'Or we could decide to be very grown-up about this thing between us—'

'*Thing?*' she put in indignantly, but his fingers were still on her face and she was shivering. And now the pad of his thumb had begun to trace a line across her lower lip and that was shivering, too.

'Desire. Lust. Whatever you want to call it. Maybe I just want to lay to rest a ghost which has haunted me for ten long years, and maybe you do, too.'

It was his candour which clinched it—the bald truth which was her undoing. He wasn't dressing up his suggestion with sentimental words which didn't mean anything. He wasn't insulting her intelligence by pretending she was the love of his life or that there was some kind of future in what he was proposing. He was saying something which had been on her mind since Michela's wedding. Because he was right. This *thing* between them wouldn't seem to go away. No matter how much she tried, she couldn't stop wanting him.

She wondered if he could read the answer in her eyes. Was that why he leaned forward to tap briefly on the glass which separated them from the driver, before taking her in his arms and starting to kiss her?

And once he had done that, she was left with no choice at all.

CHAPTER SIX

HE DIDN'T OFFER her a coffee, nor a drink. He didn't
even put the lamps on. Alannah didn't know whether
Niccolò had intended a slow seduction—but it didn't
look as if she was going to get one. Because from
the moment the front door of his Mayfair apartment
slammed shut on them, he started acting like a man
who had lost control.

His hands were in her hair, he was tugging her
coat from her shoulders so that it slid unnoticed to the
ground and his mouth was pressing down on hers. It
was breathless. It was hot. It was...*hungry*. Alannah
gasped as he caught her in his arms. He was bury-
ing his mouth in her hair and muttering urgent little
words in Sicilian and, although her Italian was good,
she didn't understand any of them. But she didn't need
to. You wouldn't have to be a linguist to understand
what Niccolò was saying to her. The raw, primitive
sounds of need were international, weren't they?

He placed his hands on either side of her hips and
drew her closer, so that she could feel the hard cra-
dle of him pressing against her. He kissed her again
and as the kiss became deeper and more urgent she
felt him moving her, until suddenly she felt the hard

surface of the wall pressed against her back and her eyelids flew open.

He drew back, his eyes blazing. 'I want you,' he said. 'I want to eat you. To suck you. To bite you. To lick you.'

She found his blatantly erotic words more than a little intimidating and momentarily she stiffened—wondering if she should confess that she wasn't very good at this. But now his palms were skating over her dress to mould the outline of her hips and the words simply wouldn't come. She felt his hand moving over her belly. She heard him suck in a ragged breath of pleasure as he began to ruck up her dress.

'Niccolò,' she said uncertainly.

'I want you,' he ground out. 'For ten years I have longed for this moment and now that it is here, I don't think I can wait a second longer.'

Niccolò closed his eyes as he reached her panties and impatiently pushed the flimsy little panel aside, because she was wet. She was very wet. He could detect the musky aroma of her sex as he slid his fingers against her heated flesh and began to move them against her with practised ease.

'Niccolò,' she whispered again.

'I want to see your breasts,' he said, moving his shaking fingers to the lapels of her silky dress and beginning to unbutton it. Within seconds two luscious mounds were revealed—their creamy flesh spilling over the edge of her bra. He narrowed his eyes to look at them. *'Madre di Dio,'* he breathed, his fingertips brushing over the soft skin. 'In the flesh it is even better. You have the most beautiful body I have ever seen.'

And suddenly he knew he really couldn't wait a second longer. Besides, she seemed more than ready for him. He felt as if something had taken hold of him and made him into someone he didn't recognise. As if this wasn't him at all but an imposter who'd entered his body. Unsteadily, he unzipped himself and he wanted to explode even before he positioned himself against her honeyed warmth.

She went very still as he entered her and for a moment he paused, afraid that he might come straight away—and when had *that* ever happened? But somehow he managed to keep it together, drawing in a deep breath and expelling it on another shuddering sigh as he began to move.

One hand was spread over her bare bottom as he hooked her legs around his hips and drove into her as if there were no tomorrow. As if there had been no yesterday. Her nails were digging into his neck as he kissed her, but he barely noticed the discomfort. He tried to hold back—to wait for her orgasm before letting go himself—but suddenly it was impossible and he knew he was going to come.

'Alannah!' he said, on a note of disbelief—and suddenly it was too late.

Wave after wave took him under. His frame was racked with spasms as he gasped out her name, caught up in a feeling so intense that he thought he might die from it. It felt like the first orgasm he'd ever had. He closed his eyes. The only orgasm he'd ever had. And it wasn't until his body had grown completely still that he noticed how silent and how still she was.

He froze.

Of course she was.

Remorse filled him as she put her hand against his chest and pushed him away. And although withdrawing from her succulent heat was the last thing he felt like doing he could see from the tight expression on her face that she wanted him to. And who could blame her?

There had been no answering cry of fulfilment from her, had there? He had given her no real *pleasure*.

With a grimace, he eased himself from her sticky warmth, bending to pull up his trousers before carefully zipping them up. 'Alannah?'

She didn't answer straight away—she was too busy fastening her dress, her fingers fumbling to slide the buttons back in place. He went to help her, but her voice was sharp.

'Don't.'

He waited until she'd finished buttoning and whatever little insect brooch she was wearing was surveying him with baleful eyes, before he lifted her chin with his finger, so that their eyes were locked on a collision course. 'I'm sorry,' he said.

She shook her head. 'It doesn't matter.'

'It does.' He heard the flatness in her voice. 'I'm not usually so...out of control.'

She gave a wry smile. 'Don't worry, Niccolò. I won't tell anyone. Your reputation is safe with me.'

His mouth hardened and his body tensed. It was her cool response which made something inside him flare into life—a feeling of anger as much as desire. A feeling set off by wounded male pride and an urgent need to put things right. This had never happened to him before. He was usually the master of control. He had always prided himself on his lovemaking skills; his ability to give women physical pleasure—even if he could never satisfy them emotionally.

A shudder of comprehension made his blood run cold.

Did he really want her to walk away thinking of him as a selfish lover? As a man who took, but gave nothing back? Was that how he wanted her to remember him?

'Let's hope you don't have to,' he said, his voice full of sudden resolution as he bent down to slide his arm behind her knees and then lifted her up.

'What...what the hell do you think you're doing?' she spluttered as he began to carry her along the wide corridor.

'I'm taking you to bed.'

'Put me down! I don't want to go to bed. I want to go home.'

'I don't think so,' he said, kicking open his bedroom door and walking over to the vast bed, before setting her down in the centre of the mattress. His knees straddling her hips, he began to unbutton her dress, but she slapped his hand away and he realised that his normal methods of seduction weren't going to work with her. Come to think of it, nothing felt remotely normal with her—and right now, this felt a million miles away from seduction.

He smoothed the tousled hair away from her face, staring down into the reproachful belligerence of her blue eyes, before slowly lowering his head to kiss her.

It wasn't a kiss, so much as a duel.

For a few seconds she held back, as if he were kissing some cold, marble statue. She lay there like a human sacrifice. He could sense her anger and frustration, so he forced himself to take it slowly—so slowly that it nearly killed him. He explored her lips with a thoroughness which was new to him—until he felt he knew them almost better than his own. And as she gradually opened them up to him—when she had relaxed enough to let his tongue slide inside her mouth—it felt like one of the most intimate acts he'd ever taken part in.

Her hands reached for his shoulders and he took the opportunity to press his body close to hers, but the shudder of delight as their bodies crushed against each other was entirely new to him. And still he took it slowly—still feasting on her lips until he was certain that her own desire was strong enough to make her wriggle against him with a wordless message of frustration.

He didn't speak. He didn't dare. Something told him that she didn't want him to undress her and he suspected that doing so would shatter a mood which was already dangerously fragile. His hands were trembling as they slid beneath her dress to reacquaint themselves with the hot, moist flesh beneath her panties. He heard her give a little moan—a sound of pleasure and submission—and his heart hammered as he unzipped himself and tugged her panties down over her knees.

He was only vaguely aware of the awkward rumpling of their unfastened clothing, because by then he was caught up with a hunger so powerful that he groaned helplessly as he slid inside her for a second time. It felt... For a moment he didn't move. It felt out of this world. He looked down to see an unmistakable flare of wonder in her eyes as he filled her, but just as quickly her dark lashes fluttered down to veil them. As if she was reluctantly granting him access to her body—but not to her thoughts.

He moved slowly. He kept her on the edge for a long time—until she was relaxed enough to let go. She wrapped her legs and her arms around him and held him close and Niccolò thought he'd never been quite so careful before. He'd learnt a lot about women's bodies during a long and comprehensive sexual education, but with Alannah it became about much more than technique.

Her body began to change. He could feel the tension building until it was stretched so tightly that it could only shatter—and when it did, she made a series of gasping little sighs, before she started to convulse helplessly around him. He was dimly aware of the groan he gave before he too let go, his every spasm matching hers, and he could feel her heart beating very fast against his as his arms tightened around her.

He must have fallen asleep, because when he next became aware of his surroundings it was to feel her shifting out from under him. His fingers curled automatically around her waist. 'What are you doing?' he questioned sleepily, moving his head so that her lips were automatically redirected to his and his voice was indistinct as his tongue slid into her mouth. 'Mmm?'

She let him kiss her for a moment before putting distance between them. He felt her lips ungluing themselves from his as she moved away.

'It's late, Niccolò—and this is a school night.'

He knew what she was doing. She was giving him

the opportunity to end the evening now, without either of them losing face. He wondered if this was what she normally did—give into a hot and mindless lust without much forethought, before following it up with a cool smile as if nothing had happened?

Without much forethought.

The words struck him and imprinted themselves on his consciousness. Suddenly he went hot and then cold as he realised their implication and he stared at her with growing horror.

'You know what we've just done?' he questioned and there was a note in his voice he'd never heard before.

She tilted her chin, but he could see the way she had instinctively started to bite her lip. 'Of course. We've just had sex. Twice.'

His fingers dug into her forearms, his voice suddenly urgent. 'Are you on the pill?'

He saw the exact moment that it registered. That would be the moment when her blue eyes widened and her lips began to tremble.

'We...' she whispered. 'We've...'

'Yes,' he completed grimly. 'We've just had unprotected sex.'

She swallowed. 'Oh, God,' she breathed. 'What are we going to do?'

He didn't answer at once. It was pointless to concentrate on the anger and frustration which were building up inside him, because he could see that harsh words of recrimination would serve no useful purpose. His mouth hardened. He should have known better. How could he have failed to take contraception into account?

'I think that there is only one thing we can do,' he said. 'We wait.'

'I...guess so.'

He frowned as he noticed that her teeth had started to chatter. 'You're shivering. You need to get into bed.'

'I don't—'

'I'm not listening to any objections,' he said emphatically. 'I'm going to undress you and put you to bed and then I'm going to make you tea.'

She wriggled. 'Why don't you go and make the tea and I'll undress myself?'

He frowned, and there was a heartbeat of a pause. 'Alannah, are you *shy*?'

She attempted a light little laugh, which didn't quite come off. 'Me? Shy? Don't be ridiculous. How could I possibly be shy when I've exposed my body to the harsh glare of the camera?'

Placing his palms on either side of her face, he stared down into her wide blue eyes. 'But stripping for a camera is a very anonymous thing to do,' he said slowly. 'While stripping for a man is intensely personal.'

She pulled a face. 'Stick with the day job, Niccolò—I don't think analysis is really your thing.'

Niccolò frowned. No, it wasn't his thing at all. Normally he ran a million miles from trying to work out what was going on in a woman's head. But most women weren't perplexing enigmas, were they? They didn't answer one question and immediately make you want to ask them a hundred more.

'You're shy,' he repeated. 'Are you going to tell me why?'

Alannah stifled a sigh as she looked at him, because telling Niccolò anything was the last thing she wanted. His lovemaking had left her feeling soft and vulnerable enough to have her defences weakened. And she wasn't stupid. She might despise the men who persisted in thinking of her as nothing but a body—yet surely that was the main attraction for Niccolò, no matter how much he might try to deny it. Wouldn't he be disappointed to discover the mundane truth about her?

Because iconic glamour models were supposed to typify sexuality, not belong to a band of women who had always found sex rather overrated until now.

'Yes, I'm shy,' she admitted grudgingly. 'I don't really like men looking at my body. I'm hung up about it. I hate being thought of as nothing but a pair of gravity-defying breasts. That's probably why I'm not usually able to relax very much. Why my sex life has been...'

Her words tailed off as she became aware that she'd said too much and she braced herself as she waited for him to distance himself, like a man who thought he'd bought a racy sports-car—only to find that he'd landed himself with a second-hand model which kept breaking down.

'Why your sex life has been, what?' he prompted softly.

She pulled a face. 'You really want me to spell it out for you? Isn't your ego healthy enough already without the added boost of me telling you how good you are in bed?'

He took her hand and lifted it to his lips, unable to hide his slow, curving smile of satisfaction. 'Am I?'

'You know you are.' She pulled her hand away. 'I'm sure I'm not the first woman to tell you that.'

'No, but you're the first woman who is such a mass of contradictions that you have my head spinning. You have a wildness...'

'Niccolò—'

He silenced her with a long kiss and when he finally raised his head, it was to subject her to a look of narrow-eyed thoughtfulness. 'I think we've done the subject to death for tonight,' he said. 'You're tired and so am I, and you're right—it *is* a school night. Bedtime,' he added firmly.

'I'm not sure,' she said.

'Well, I am. Relax, *mia tentatrice.*'

He was unbuttoning her dress again and suddenly Alannah had no desire to stop him. She lay there as he slid the silky garment from her body until she was left in just her hold-ups and her bra and, automatically, her palms moved towards her breasts—to protect them from his seeking gaze. But to her surprise he wasn't even looking at her breasts. He was sliding down her hold-ups as impersonally as if he'd been undressing a child who had been caught in a storm. Even her bra was removed with nothing but deft efficiency, so that she was naked and snuggled beneath the warm duvet almost before she'd realised it.

She blinked as he captured her in that searing ebony gaze.

'Now...was that so traumatic?' he questioned silkily.

She shook her head. 'I wasn't expecting...' Her words tailed off.

'You thought I would be unable to resist drooling

as I ogled your breasts? That you find yourself surprised by my sensitivity?'

'Something like that,' she mumbled.

He smiled, the pad of his thumb trailing a path over her bottom lip and causing it to tremble. 'You and me both,' he said drily, before getting up to let himself quietly out of the room.

While he was gone, Alannah took the opportunity to look around what was one of the most impersonal bedrooms she'd ever seen. There were no photos on display. No real hints as to what kind of man Niccolò really was. She knew his parents were dead—but there was no misty-eyed memorial of their wedding day. She remembered Michela clamming up whenever anyone had asked her about her folks—and hadn't she been a bit like that herself if people wanted to know about *her* father? It had seemed too crass to tell them the truth. *Oh, my mother was fresh out of Ireland and she had her drink spiked...*

She hadn't found out the whole story until three days before her mother had died. That Bridget Collins had woken up in her dingy hostel room with a splitting headache and vague, shifting memories of what had happened the night before—as well as a terrible soreness between her legs. She'd never seen the man again and the shame of it was that she didn't even know his surname. Nine months later Alannah had been born and her mother's over-protectiveness had kicked in.

Alannah stared at the photograph opposite the bed—a smoky, atmospheric monochrome study of a brooding Mount Vesuvius. If she'd known all that stuff before...if she'd been able to make sense of why

her mother had been so unbelievably strict with her—
would it have changed anything?

Probably not. And even if it had—it was all irrel-
evant now. Because you could never go back. You
could never wipe out the things you'd done. Everyone knew that.

She was almost asleep by the time Niccolò returned, carrying a tray of camomile tea. Her eye-
lashes fluttered open as he sat down and the bed sank
beneath his weight.

'This will help you sleep,' he said.

She didn't think she needed any help, but she drank
the flower-filled brew anyway and then settled back
down against the bank of pillows while Niccolò gently
stroked her hair.

She wriggled her bare toes and stretched out her
body and at that precise moment she didn't think
she'd ever felt quite so blissfully content. Until a dark
memory flickered into her mind like an evil imp—
reinforcing the disturbing thought that they hadn't
remembered to use protection....

CHAPTER SEVEN

'ANYONE WOULD THINK,' said Niccolò slowly, 'that you were trying to avoid me.'

Alannah looked up to find herself caught in the spotlight of a pair of ebony eyes, which cut into her like dark twin lasers. Winter light was flooding into the main reception room of the still bare Sarantos apartment, emphasising its vast and elegant dimensions. She had been there all morning, sitting on the newly upholstered window seat and sewing tassels onto a cushion, but the sight of the Sicilian standing in the doorway made her suspend her needle in mid-air.

She tried to compose herself and to say the right thing. Just as she'd been trying to do the right thing, ever since she'd crazily decided to have sex with him. She needed to treat what had happened as a one-off, and keeping their relationship on a purely professional footing was the only sane solution.

For both of them.

She put the needle down and pushed her empty coffee mug along the floor with the tip of her sneaker. 'Of course I'm not trying to avoid you,' she said lightly. 'You're my boss—I wouldn't dare.'

'Is that so?' He walked towards her. 'So why wouldn't you have dinner with me last night?'

'I explained that,' she protested. 'I had to travel to Somerset to buy some paintings and the man who owned the shop was just about to close up for the holidays, so it was the only day I could go. And then on the way back, there were loads of leaves on the line so the train was delayed. Didn't you get my voicemail message?'

'Oh, yes, I got your voicemail message,' he said impatiently. He stood looking down at her, feeling perplexed and more than a little frustrated. This had never happened to him before. Usually he had to barricade his bedroom once a woman had been granted access to it—he couldn't remember a lover ever being so reluctant to return. His mouth tightened. 'But the fact remains that on Tuesday we had sex and I've barely seen you since.'

She shrugged. 'That's just the way it's worked out. You're employing me to get this apartment done in a hurry and that's what I'm trying to do. That's my primary role, isn't it? You're not paying me to keep appearing at your office door and haunting you.'

Niccolò felt his mouth dry. He wouldn't mind her appearing at his office door. She was making him think of a few very creative uses for his desk... He swallowed. 'Am I going to see you later?'

Alannah sucked in a breath, trying not to be flattered at his persistence, but it wasn't easy. Because she had been dreading this meeting. Dreading and yet longing for it, all at the same time. Ever since she'd slipped out of his Mayfair apartment on Tuesday she'd told herself that it would be safer to stay away from Niccolò and not pursue the affair any further. She liked him. She liked him way more than was sensible for what she was sure he'd only ever intended to be a casual hook-up. And she didn't do casual. Just as she didn't do the kind of affair which would end up with her getting her heart smashed into a hundred little pieces.

'You're my boss, Niccolò,' she said.

'I haven't lost sight of that fact, *mia tentatrice*. But what does that have to do with anything?'

'You know very well. It's…unprofessional.'

He gave a soft laugh. 'You don't think we might already have crossed that boundary when you lay gasping underneath me for most of the night?' He narrowed his eyes. 'And on top of me at one point, if my memory serves me well.'

'Stop it,' she whispered, feeling colour flooding into her cheeks. 'That's exactly what I'm talking about. It blurs the lines and confuses things. I'm trying to concentrate on my work and I can't when you—'

'Can't stop wanting a rerun?'

'A rerun is what you do with movies. And it's a bad idea.'

'Why?'

She sighed. 'What happened last week was…' Her words tailed off. How best to describe it? The most amazing sex she'd ever had? Well, yes. She had certainly never realised it could be so intense, or so powerful. But there had been another blissful side to that night which was far more worrying. She'd realised that she could get used to waking up with Niccolò lying asleep beside her, his arms wrapped tightly around her. Just as she could get used to thinking about him at odd moments of the day and wishing he were there to kiss her. And those kind of daydreams would get her nowhere.

Because where would that leave her when the whole thing imploded? She'd just be another heart-broken woman crying into her gin and tonic, trying to resist the urge to send him a 'casual' late-night text. She would run the risk of making herself vulnerable and she wasn't going to let that happen. She felt a new resolve steal over her. 'A mistake,' she said.

'A mistake,' he repeated.

'Maybe that's a bad way to put it. It was obviously very enjoyable.' She pushed the cushion away and forced herself to face the truth, no matter how un-palatable it was. 'But the fact remains that you don't really like me. You told me that.'

He smiled. 'I like you a lot more now.'

'You described what you felt for me as, and I quote—"a wildness". You made me sound like a mild version of the bubonic plague.'

'I don't think any plague feels quite like this—ex-cept maybe for the fever in my blood when I close my eyes at night and find it impossible to sleep because I can't get you out of my mind.' His eyes gleamed. 'And you look incredibly beautiful when you're being defiant. Do you do it because you know how much it turns me on?'

'It's not defiance for the sake of it,' she said. 'It's defiance for a reason. I'm not doing it to try to entice you.' She forced herself to say it. To put the words out there instead of having them nagging away in-side her. 'This relationship isn't going anywhere. We both know that.'

'So you're not pregnant?'

His words completely shattered her fragile façade and she stared at him, her heart pounding. During the day, when she was busy working, it was easy to push that thought to the back of her mind. It was at night-time when it became impossible. That was when the fear flooded through her body as she tried to imagine just how she would cope with having Niccolò da Conti's baby. That was when she had to fight to stop herself imagining a downy little black head, glugging away contentedly at her breast.

'I don't know,' she said. 'It's too early to do a test.'

'Which means we may be about to be parents to-gether, *si*? I think that constitutes some sort of relationship, don't you?'

'Not the best kind,' she said.

'Maybe not. But I need to know that if you are pregnant—*if you are*—whether I am the only man in the frame who could be the father.' His black eyes burned into her, but he must have seen her flinch because his voice softened by a fraction. 'Is that such an unreasonable request?'

She met his gaze, telling herself that in the circumstances he had every right to ask. But that didn't make it hurt any less and some of that hurt came spilling out.

'Yes. You are the only man in the frame. Did you think that because of my previous line of work that there would be a whole load of contenders?' She shook her head in despair. 'You really are fond of stereotypes, aren't you, Niccolò? Well, for your information, there isn't. If you really must know, I could count my previous lovers on one hand and still have some fingers free—and there's been no one in my life for the last three years.'

Niccolò let out the breath he'd been holding, unprepared for the powerful hit of pleasure which flooded through his body in response to her words. *He was the only man in the frame. There had been no one else in her life for the past three years.*

He stared at her, his eyes taking in the way she was illuminated in the harsh winter light. Her thick hair looked blue-black, like the feathers of a raven. He swallowed. *Dai capelli corvini.*

In her jeans and loose shirt she shouldn't have looked anything special, but somehow she looked unbelievably beautiful. Against her hair, her skin was creamy and her pallor emphasised the dramatic blue of her eyes. A little brooch in the shape of a dragonfly glittered on her lapel and suddenly he found himself envying the proximity of that worthless piece of jewellery to her body.

What if there were a baby?

His mouth hardened.

He would cross that bridge when he came to it.

The shrill sound of the doorbell shattered the silence.

'That'll be one of the painters,' she said. 'He rang up to say he'd left his keys behind.' Rising to her feet, she walked over and picked up a shoal of silver keys from where they lay on another window seat. 'I won't be long.'

Alannah was aware of his eyes burning into her as she left the room. Her shoes were squeaking as she went to open the front door where one of the painters stood. There were four of them in total and they'd been working around the clock—and although she'd stopped short of making cups of tea for them, she'd been friendly enough. This one had plaster dust in his hair and he was grinning.

She forced a smile as she held out the clump of keys. 'Here you go, Gary.'

But after he'd taken them and shoved them into his dust-covered jeans, he caught hold of her wrist. His big, calloused fingers curled around her skin and his face had suddenly gone very pink. 'I didn't realise you were *the* Alannah Collins,' he said suddenly.

Her heart sank as she snatched her hand away because she knew what was coming next. She wondered if it would be better to call his bluff or to slam the door in his face. But there were only a few days of the project left and it *was* nearly Christmas...why alienate one of the workforce unless it was absolutely necessary?

'Will there be anything else?' she questioned pointedly. 'Because I have work to do.'

'The schoolgirl,' he said thickly. 'With the big—'

A figure seemed to propel itself out of nowhere and it took a moment for Alannah to realise it was Niccolò and he was launching himself at Gary with a look of undiluted rage on his face.

Grabbing hold of the workman's shirt collar, he half lifted him from the ground and shoved his face very close.

'*Che talii bastardu?*' he spat out. '*Ti scippo locchi e o core!*'

'Niccolò!' protested Alannah faintly, but he didn't seem to be listening.

'How dare you speak to a woman like that?' he demanded. 'What's your name?'

The man blanched. 'G-Gary.'

'Gary what?'

'G-Gary Harkness.'

'Well, take it from me that you won't ever work in this city again, Gary Harkness—I shall make sure of that.' Releasing the shirt collar, Niccolò pushed him away and the man staggered a little. 'Now get out of here—get out before I beat your worthless body to a piece of pulp.'

Alannah didn't think she'd ever seen anyone look so petrified as the workman turned and ran down the corridor towards the elevator.

She lifted her gaze to Niccolò and met the furious blaze firing from his eyes as he clicked the door shut.

'What was that you said to him in Sicilian?'

'I asked him what he was looking at.' He paused as he steadied his breath. 'And I told him I would wrench out his eyes and his heart.'

Alannah gulped. 'You don't think that was a lit-tle...over the top?'

'I think he's lucky he didn't end up in hospital,' he ground out and his jaw tightened as he stared at her. 'How often does that happen?'

'Not much. Not these days.' She shrugged as she began to walk back into the main reception room, aware that he was following her. Aware that her heart was pounding. This wasn't a conversation she usually had—not with anyone—but maybe Niccolò was someone who needed to hear it. She turned to look at him. 'It used to be a lot worse. People only ever seemed able to have a conversation with my breasts—

or think that I would instantly want to fall into bed with them.'

Guilt whispered over his skin and Niccolò swallowed down the sudden dryness in his throat. Because hadn't he done something very similar? Hadn't he judged her without really knowing the facts and assumed a promiscuity which simply wasn't true?

'And I did the same,' he said slowly.

Her gaze was fearless. 'Yes, you did.'

'That was why you suddenly froze in the hallway of my house when I was making love to you, wasn't it?' he questioned suddenly.

His perception was nearly as alarming as the realisation that the conversation had taken an even more intimate twist. Despite her determination to stay strong, Alannah couldn't prevent the rush of heat to her cheeks. 'Yes,' she said quietly.

She started to turn her head away, but suddenly he was right there in front of her and his fingers were on her arm. They felt good on her arm, she thought inconsequentially.

'Tell me,' he urged.

It was hard to get the words out. Baring her soul wasn't something she normally did—and she had never imagined herself confiding in Niccolò da Conti like this. But for once his gaze was understanding and his voice was soft and Alannah found herself wanting to analyse the way she'd reacted—not just because he'd asked, but because she needed to make sense of it herself. 'I just remember you saying something about my body being even better in the flesh and I started to feel like an object. Like I wasn't a real person—

just a two-dimensional image in a magazine, with a staple in her navel. Like I was *invisible*.'

'That was not my intention,' he said slowly. 'I think I found myself overwhelmed by the realisation that I was finally making love to you after so many years of thinking about it.' There was a pause as he looked at her. 'Do you think you can forgive me for that, *mia tentatrice*?'

She studied him, and the flicker of a smile nudged at her lips because it was strange seeing him in this conciliatory mood. 'I'll think about it.'

Niccolò pulled her into his arms and she didn't object. She didn't object when he bent his head to kiss her either. Her breath was warm and flavoured with coffee and he wanted to groan with pleasure. She tasted as good as he remembered—in fact, she tasted even better—and there seemed something awfully decadent about kissing her in the near-empty apartment. This wasn't the kind of thing he usually did between meetings, was it? His heart skipped a beat as his fingertips skated over her breast, feeling it swell as he cupped it, and he heard her breath quicken as he began to unbutton her shirt.

It pleased him that she let him. That she really did seem to have forgiven him for his out-of-control behaviour of the other night. That she was relaxed enough not to freeze again.

He deepened the kiss, rubbing at her taut nipple with his thumb, and she gave a little sigh of pleasure. He kissed her for a long time until she was squirming impatiently and kissing him back. Until he forced himself to pull away from her, his voice unsteady as he looked into the darkening of her denim eyes and he felt a rush of triumph fuse with the headiness of sexual hunger.

'I would like to lay you down on the bare floor and make love to you, but I am short of time and must go straight from here to a meeting. And I don't feel it would do my reputation much good if I walked in so dishevelled.' He grimaced as he remembered that time in the hallway of his apartment, when he had shown all the finesse of a teenage boy. 'And I am aware that perhaps you like your lovemaking to be a little more slow and considered.'

'I...thought I did.'

He heard the reluctance in her voice but noticed she was still gripping tightly onto his arms. Her lips were trembling, even though she was biting down on them in an effort to stop it—and he realised just how turned on she was.

'Of course...' He moved his hand down to the ridge of hard denim between her legs. 'I probably do have enough time for other things. Things which you might enjoy.'

'Niccolò,' she said breathlessly.

'What do you think?' he said as he edged his middle finger forward and began to stroke her. 'Yes, or no?'

'Y-yes,' she gasped.

'Keep still,' he urged—but to his delight she didn't obey him. Or maybe she just couldn't. Her head was tipping back and suddenly she didn't look remotely shy...she looked *wild*. Beautiful. He felt her thighs part and heard her moaning softly as he increased the relentless pressure of his finger.

She came very quickly, tightening her arms around

his neck and making that shuddering little crescendo of sighs with which he'd become so familiar on Tuesday night. As he kissed her again her fingers began to claw at his shirt, as if she wanted to tear it from his chest, and for a moment he thought about changing his mind and taking her in the most fundamental way possible.

Temptation rushed over him in a dark wave. Impatiently, his hand strayed to the belt of his trousers, until some remaining shred of reason forced him to play out the ensuring scene. What did he have in mind? Rushing into his meeting with his shirt creased and a telltale flush darkening his skin? Using Alekto's apartment to have sex with a woman—wouldn't that be kind of *cheap*? On every single level, it wouldn't work—but that didn't make it any easier to pull away from her.

She started buttoning her shirt back up with trembling fingers and he walked over to the window to compose himself, willing his frustration to subside.

Outside, a light flurry of snowflakes was whirling down and he felt a sudden sense of restlessness. He thought about the impending holiday and what he would be forced to endure, because one thing he'd learned was that unless you were prepared to live in a cave—it was impossible to ignore Christmas. Already there was a glittering tree which he'd been unable to ban from the main reception of his offices. He thought about the horrendous staff party he'd been forced to attend last night, with those stodgy mince pies they were so fond of eating and several drunken secretaries tottering over to him with glassy smiles and bunches of mistletoe.

He turned round. Alannah had finished buttoning up her shirt, though he noticed her hands were shaking and her cheeks still flushed.

'What are you doing for Christmas?' he questioned suddenly.

'Oh, I'm wavering between an invitation to eat nut roast with some committed vegans, or having an alternative celebration all of my own.' She glanced over his shoulder at the snowflakes. 'Like pretending that nothing's happening and eating beans on toast, followed by an overdose of chocolate and trash TV. What about you?'

He shrugged. 'I have an invitation to ski with some friends in Klosters, but unfortunately my schedule doesn't allow it. I hate Christmas. What I would really like is to fast-forward the calendar and wake up to find it was the new year.'

'Oh, dear,' she said softly.

His eyes met hers and another wave of desire washed over him. 'But since we are both at a loose end, it seems a pity not to capitalise on that. We could ignore the seasonal madness and just please ourselves.'

She opened her eyes very wide. 'Are you asking me to spend Christmas with you, Niccolò?'

There was a pause. 'It seems I am.' He gave a cool smile. 'So why don't you speak to Kirsty and have her give you one of my credit cards? You can book us into the best suite in the best hotel in the city—somewhere you've always wanted to stay. Forget the nut roast and the beans on toast—you can have as much caviar and champagne as you like.' He gave a slow smile as he touched his fingertips to her raven hair. 'Maybe I can make some of your Christmas wishes come true.'

* * *

Alannah felt like taking her sharpest pair of scissors and snipping the small square of plastic into tiny pieces. She thought about what Niccolò had said to her. Make her wishes come true. *Really?* Did he honestly think that staying in a fancy hotel suite was the sum total of her life's ambition, when right now her biggest wish would be to tell him that she didn't need his fancy platinum credit card and she'd rather spend Christmas day alone than spend it with him?

Except that it wouldn't be true, would it? She might *want* it to be true, but it wasn't. Why else would she be sitting hunched in front of her computer, about to book a two-night break in a London hotel? She wondered what had happened to her determination to forget the night she'd spent with him and maintain a professional relationship.

She bit her lip. It had been shattered by Niccolò's resolve—that was what had happened. She had been lost the moment he'd kissed her. A single touch had been enough to make all her good intentions crumble. All her silent vows had been a complete waste of time—because she'd gone up in flames the moment he'd taken her in his arms.

She remembered the way his fingertip had whispered over the crotch of her jeans and her face grew hot. She hadn't been so shy then, had she? He'd soon had her bucking beneath him, and he hadn't even had to remove a single item of clothing. And still in that dreamy, post-orgasmic state she had agreed to spend Christmas with him.

That was something it was hard to get her head round. There must be millions of things he could be doing for the holiday—but he wanted to spend it with her. *Her.* Didn't that mean something? Her mouth grew dry. Surely it *had* to.

She stared at the credit card, which Kirsty had crisply informed her had no upper limit. Imagine that. Imagine having enough money to buy whatever you wanted. *The best suite in the best hotel.* How fancy would a hotel have to be for Niccolò not to have seen it all before, and be jaded by it? She ran through a list of possibilities. The Savoy. The Ritz. The Granchester. London had heaps of gorgeous hotels and she'd bet that he'd stayed in all of them. Had constant exposure to high-end affluence helped contribute to his inbuilt cynicism?

She was just about to click onto the Granchester when something made her hesitate. Perhaps it was a desire to shift him out of his comfort zone—away from the usual protective barriers which surrounded him. He had knocked down some of her defences, so why shouldn't she do the same with him? Why *shouldn't* she try to find out more about the real Niccolò da Conti?

She thought of a fancy hotel dining room and all the other people who would be congregated there. People who had no real place to go, who just wanted the holiday to be over. Or even worse—the wink-wink attitude of Room Service if they started asking for turkey sandwiches and champagne to be brought to their room.

An idea popped into her mind and it started to grow more attractive by the minute. She stared at the long number on the credit card. She might not have much money of her own, but she did have her imagination. Surely she was capable of surprising him with something unexpected. Something simple yet meaningful, which would incorporate the true meaning of Christmas.

His power and privilege always gave him an edge of superiority and that couldn't be good for him. An expensive tab in a smart hotel would only reinforce the differences between them. Wouldn't it be great to feel more like his *equal* for a change?

Because what if she *was* pregnant? She was going to have to get to know him better, no matter what the outcome. Her heart gave a painful lurch as she waited for that intrusive yet strangely compelling image of Niccolò da Conti's baby to subside.

She waited a minute before typing *cute Christmas cottage* into her browser. Because cute was exactly what she needed right now, she told herself. Cute stood a chance of making a cynical man melt so you might be able to work out what made him tick. Scrolling down, she stared at the clutch of country cottages which appeared on the screen.

Perfect.

CHAPTER EIGHT

THE FLURRIES WERE getting stronger and Niccolò cursed as he headed along the narrow country lane.

Why could nothing ever be straightforward? Glancing in his rear-view mirror at the swirl of snowflakes which was obscuring his view, he scowled. He'd given Alannah a credit card and told her to book a hotel in town and she'd done the exact opposite—directing him to some godforsaken spot deep in the countryside, while she went on ahead earlier.

Well, in terms of distance he wasn't actually *that* far from London but he might as well be in middle of his friend Murat's Qurhahian desert for all the sense he could make of his bearings. The sudden onset of heavy snow had made the world look like an alien place and it was difficult to get his bearings. Familiar landmarks had disappeared. The main roads were little more than white wastelands and the narrow lanes had begun to resemble twisting snakes of snow.

Glancing at his satnav, he could see he was only four minutes away, but he was damned if he could see any hotel. He'd passed the last chocolate-boxy village some way back and now an arrow was indicating he take the left fork in the road, through an impenetra-ble-looking line of trees.

Still cursing, he turned off the road, his powerful headlights illuminating the swirling snowflakes and turning them golden. Some people might have considered the scene pretty, but he wasn't in the mood for pretty scenery. He wanted a drink, a shower and sex in exactly that order and he wanted them now.

Following the moving red arrow, he drove slowly until at last he could see a lighted building in the distance, but it looked too small to be a hotel. His mouth hardened. Something that small could only ever be described as a cottage.

He could see a thatched roof covered with a thick dusting of snow and an old-fashioned lamp lit outside a front door, on which hung a festive wreath of holly and ivy. Through latticed windows a woman was moving around—her fall of raven hair visible, even from this distance. His hands tightened around the steering wheel as he brought the car to a halt and got out—his shoes sinking noiselessly into the soft, virgin carpet.

He rang the bell—one of those old-fashioned bells you only ever saw on ships, or in movies. He could hear the sudden scurrying of movement and footsteps approaching and then the door opened and Alannah stood there, bathed in muted rainbow light.

His body tensing, he stepped inside and the door swung violently shut behind him. His senses were immediately bombarded by the scene in front of him but, even so, the first thing he noticed was her dress. Who could fail to notice a dress like that?

It wasn't so much the golden silk, which skimmed

her curves and made her look like a living treasure, it was the scooped neck showing unfamiliar inches of creamy skin and the soft swell of her breasts. She had even positioned the glittery grasshopper brooch so that it looked poised to hop straight onto her nipple. Had she started to relax enough to stop covering her body up in that old puritanical way? he wondered.

But even this wasn't enough to hold his attention for long. His gaze moved behind her, where a fire was blazing—with two wing chairs on either side. Sprigs of holly had been placed above the paintings and, yes, there was the inevitable sprig of mistletoe dangling from the ceiling. On a low table a bowl was filled with clementines and in the air he could scent something cooking, rich with the scent of cinnamon and spice. But it was the Christmas tree which jarred most. A fresh fir tree with coloured lights looped all over the fragrant branches from which hung matching baubles of gold.

He flinched, but she didn't seem to notice as she wound her arms around his neck and positioned her lips over his. 'Merry Christmas,' she whispered.

Like a drowning man he fought against her feminine softness and the faint drift of pomegranate which clung to her skin. Disentangling her arms, he took a step back as he felt the clutch of ice around his heart.

'What's going on?' he questioned.

She blinked, as if something in his voice had alerted her to the fact that all was not well. 'It's a surprise.'

'I don't like surprises.'

Her eyes now held a faint sense of panic. Was she realising just how wrong she'd got it? he wondered grimly. He could see her licking her lips and the anger inside him seemed to bubble and grow.

'I thought about booking a hotel in London,' she said quickly. 'But I thought you'd probably stayed in all those places before, or somewhere like them. And then I thought about creating a real Christmas, right here in the countryside.'

'A *real* Christmas,' he repeated slowly.

'That's right.' She gestured towards a box of truffles on the table, as if the sight of chocolate were going to make him have a sudden change of heart. 'I went online at Selfridges and ordered a mass of stuff from their food hall. It was still much cheaper than a hotel. That's a ham you can smell cooking and I've bought fish too, because I know in Europe you like to eat fish at Christmas. Oh, and mince pies, of course.'

'I hate mince pies.'

'You don't…' Her voice faltered, as if she could no longer ignore the harsh note of censure in his voice. 'You don't *have* to eat them.'

'I hate Christmas, full stop,' he said viciously. 'I already told you that, Alannah—so which part of the sentence did you fail to understand?'

Her fingers flew over her lips and, with the silky dress clinging to her curves, she looked so like a medieval damsel in distress that he was momentarily tempted to pull her into his arms and blot out everything with sex.

But only momentarily. Because then he looked up and saw the Christmas angel on top of the tree and something about those gossamer-fine wings made his heart clench with pain. He felt the walls of the tiny cottage closing in on him as a dark tide of unwanted emotion washed over him.

'Which part, Alannah?' he repeated.

She held out the palms of her hands in a gesture of appeal. 'I thought—'

'What did you think?' he interrupted savagely. 'That you could treat me like your tame puppet? Playing happy couples around the Christmas tree and indulging in some happy-ever-after fantasy, just because we've had sex and I asked to spend the holidays with you, since we were both at a loose end?'

'Actually,' she said, walking over to the blaze of the fire and turning back to stare at him, 'I thought about how soulless it might be—having a corporate Christmas in some horrible anonymous hotel. I thought that with the kind of life you lead, you might like some home cooking for a change.'

'But I don't *do* home. Don't you get that?' he questioned savagely. He saw a small, rectangular present lying on the table and realised he hadn't even bought her a gift. *It wasn't supposed to be that kind of Christmas.* He shook his head. 'I can't stay here, Alannah. I'm sorry if you've gone to a lot of trouble but it's going to be wasted. So pack everything up while I put out the fire. We're going back to town.'

'No,' she said quietly.

His eyes narrowed. 'What do you mean...*no*?'

'You go if you want to, but I'm staying here.'

There was a pause. 'On your own?'

Alannah felt a sudden kick of rebellion as she met the incredulity in his eyes. 'You find that so surprising?' she demanded. 'You think I'm scared? Well, think again, Niccolò. I live on my own. I've spent pretty much the last seven years on my own. I don't need a man to protect me and look after me—and I certainly don't want to drive back to London with someone who can misinterpret a simple gesture with your kind of cynicism. So go to your anonymous hotel and spend the next few days splashing your cash and telling yourself how much you hate Christmas. I'll be perfectly happy here with my chocolate and mulled wine.'

His black eyes glittered. 'I'm telling you now that if you're calling my bluff, it won't work. I'm not staying here, but I'm not leaving without you, either.'

'I'm afraid you don't have a choice,' she said, walking across to the cocktail cabinet and pouring herself a glass of wine with a trembling hand. 'Like I said, I'm not going anywhere—and I don't imagine that even you are macho enough to drag me out by my hair. So leave. Go on. Just *leave*!'

Silently, they faced each other off before he pulled open the door and a fierce gust of wind brought a great flurry of snowflakes whirling into the room, before it slammed shut behind him.

Alannah didn't move as she heard the sound of his car starting up and then slowly pulling away on the snowy path. Her fingers tightened around her wine glass as she wondered how she could have judged him so badly. Had she thought that, because he'd murmured soft words in Sicilian when he'd been deep inside her, he'd lost the elements of ruthlessness and control which defined him?

Or was he right? Had she been naïve enough to imagine that a homespun meal might make him crave an intimacy which extended beyond the bedroom?

Her heart pounded.

Yes, she had.

Walking over to the sink, she threw away the wine, washing out the glass and putting it on the side to dry. She drew the curtains on the snowy darkness of the night and switched on the radio, just in time to hear the traditional Christmas service being broadcast from King's College, Cambridge. And as soon as the sound of carols filled the room she felt tears spring to her eyes, because it was so heartbreakingly beautiful.

She thought about the nativity scene—the helpless little child in a manger, and briefly she closed her eyes. She'd got it so wrong, hadn't she? She had taken him as her lover and ignored all the warning bells which had sounded so loudly in her ears. She had conveniently forgotten that everything was supposed to be on *his* terms and she'd tried to turn it into something it wasn't. Something it could never be. What had she been thinking of? She'd even bought herself a new and more revealing dress to send out the silent message that he had liberated her from some of her inhibitions. And she was almost as grateful to him for that as she was about the job he'd given her.

But he had thrown the offer back in her face.

She was cold now and ran upstairs to find a sweater, her heart contracting painfully as she looked around the bedroom. She had thought he would be charmed by the antique iron bedstead and the broderie-anglais linen. She'd imagined him picking up that old-fashioned jug and studying it—or telling her that he liked the view out into the snow-covered woods at the back of the house. She had planned to run him a bath when he arrived, and to light some of the scented candles she'd had delivered from London. She had pictured washing his back. Maybe even joining him, if he could persuade her to do so. She'd never shared a bath with anyone before.

What a fool she was, she thought viciously, dragging a mismatched blue sweater over the golden dress, and shaking her hair free. It wasn't as if she'd had no experience of life and the cruel lessons it could teach you. Hadn't she learnt that you had to just accept what you were given—warts and all? She should have taken what was already on the table and been satisfied with that. But she had been greedy, hadn't she? Niccolò had offered her something, but it hadn't been enough. She had wanted more. And still more.

The sound of the front door clicking open and closing again made her heart race with a sudden fear which made a mockery of her defiant words to Niccolò. Why the hell hadn't she locked it after he'd left—or was she hoping to extend an open invitation to any passing burglar? Except that no self-respecting burglar would be out on a snowy Christmas Eve like this. Even burglars probably had someone to share the holiday with.

'Who is it?' she called.

'Who do you think it is? Father Christmas?'

The sardonic Sicilian voice echoed round the small cottage and Alannah went to the top of the stairs to see Niccolò standing in the sitting room, snow clinging like frozen sugar to his black hair and cashmere coat. He looked up.

'It's me,' he said.

'I can see that. What happened?' she questioned

sarcastically as she began to walk downstairs. 'Did you change your mind about the mince pies?'

He was pulling off his coat and snow was falling in little white showers to the ground. She reached the bottom stair just as the poignant strains of 'Silent Night' poured from the radio. Quickly, she turned it off, so that all she could hear was the crackling of the fire and the sound of her own heartbeat as she stared at him. 'Why did you come back?'

There was a pause. His black eyes became suddenly hooded. 'It's a filthy night. I couldn't face leaving you here on your own.'

'And I told you that I would be fine. I'm not scared of the dark.' *I'm much more scared of the way you make me feel when you kiss me.*

'I'm not about to change my mind,' he said. 'I'm staying, and I need a drink.'

'Help yourself.'

He walked over to the bottle she'd opened earlier. 'You?'

A drink would choke me. 'No, thanks.'

She went and sat by the fire, wondering how she was going to get through the next few hours. How the hell did you pass the time when you were stuck somewhere with someone who didn't want to be there? After a couple of moments Niccolò walked over and handed her a glass of wine, but she shook her head.

'I said I didn't want one.'

'Take it, Alannah. Your face is pale.'

'My face is always pale.' But she took it anyway and drank a mouthful as he sat down in the other chair. 'And you still haven't really told me why you came back.'

Niccolò drank some of his wine and for a moment he said nothing. His natural instinct would be to tell her that he didn't have to justify his actions to her. To anyone. But something strange had happened as he'd driven his car down the snowy lane. Instead of the freedom he'd been expecting, he had felt nothing but a heavy weight settling somewhere deep in his chest. It had occurred to him that he could go and stay in a hotel. That if the truth were known, he could easily get a flight and join his friends and their skiing party. He could pretty much get a plane to anywhere, because the hosts of the many parties he'd declined would have been delighted if he'd turned up unexpectedly.

But then he'd thought of Alannah. Curled up alone by the fire with her raven hair aglow, while beside her that corny Christmas tree glittered. All that trouble she'd taken to create some sort of occasion and he'd just callously thrown it back in her face. What kind of a man did that? He thought of how much he'd anticipated making love to her again. How he'd spent the day aching to possess her and wanting to feel her arms wrapped tightly around him. What was *wrong* with him?

He put down his glass and his face was sombre as he turned to look at her.

'I came back because I realised I was behaving like an idiot,' he said. 'I shouldn't have taken it out on you and I'm sorry.'

Alannah sensed that sorry wasn't a word which usually featured highly in his vocabulary, but she wasn't letting him off that lightly. Did he think that a single word could wash away all the hurt he'd inflicted? 'But you did.'

'Yes. I did.'

'Because you always have to be in charge don't you, Niccolò?' she demanded, her anger starting to bubble up. 'You decided how you wanted Christmas to play out and that was it as far as you were concerned. What *you* want is paramount, and everyone else's wishes can just go hang. This is exactly what happened at Michela's wedding, isn't it? Niccolò wants it this way—so this is the way it must be.'

'That was different.'

'How?' she demanded. 'How was it different? How did you ever get to be so damned...*controlling*?'

The flames were flickering over his brooding features and illuminating his ebony hair, so that it glowed like fire-touched coal.

'How?' He gave a short laugh. 'You don't have any ideas?'

'Because you're Sicilian?'

'But I'm not,' he said unexpectedly. 'I'm only half Sicilian. My blood is not "pure". I am half Corsican.' He frowned. 'You didn't know that?'

She shook her head and suddenly his almost swashbuckling appearance made sense. 'No. I had no idea. Michela never really talked about that kind of thing. Boarding school is about reinvention—and escape. About painting yourself in the best possible light so that nobody feels sorry for you. All we knew was that you were unbelievably strict.' She put her glass down. 'Although you did used to take her to the Bahamas for Christmas every year, and we used to get pretty jealous about that.'

'She never told you why?'

'I knew that your parents were dead.' She hesitated. 'But nobody wants to talk about that kind of stuff, do they?'

Niccolò felt his mouth dry. No, they didn't. They definitely didn't. And when death was connected with shame, it made you want to turn your back on it even more. To keep it hidden. To create some kind of distance and move as far away from it as you could. He'd done that for Michela, but he'd done it for himself, too. Because some things were easier to forget than to remember.

Yet even though she was doing her best to disguise it, Alannah was looking at him with such hurt and confusion on her face that he felt it stab at his conscience. All she'd done was to try to make his Christmas good and he had thrown it back in her face in a way she didn't deserve. He'd given her a lot of stuff she didn't deserve, he realised—and didn't he owe her some kind of explanation?

'Mine was a very…unusual upbringing,' he said, at last. 'My mother came from a powerful Sicilian family who disowned her when she married my father.'

She raised her eyebrows. 'Wasn't that a little… dramatic?'

He shrugged. 'Depends which point of view you take. Her family was one of the wealthiest on the island—and my father was an itinerant Corsican with a dodgy background, who worked in the kitchens of one of her family hotels. It was never going to be thought of as an ideal match—not by any stretch of the imagination.' His gaze fixed on the flames which danced around one of the logs. 'My father was completely uneducated but he possessed a tremendous charisma.' He gave a bitter laugh. 'Along with a massive gambling addiction and a love of the finer things in life. My mother told me that her parents did everything in their power to prevent the marriage and when they couldn't—they told her she would only ever be welcome if she parted from him. Which for a strictly traditional Sicilian family was a pretty big deal.'

Alannah stared at him. 'So what did she do?'

'She defied them and married him anyway. She loved him. And she let that *love*—' His voice took the word and distorted it—so that when it left his lips it sounded like something dark and savage. 'She let it blind her to everything. His infidelity. His habitual absences. The fact that he was probably more in love with her inheritance, than with her. They took the boat to Italy when my mother was pregnant with me and we lived in some style in Rome—while my father flew to casinos all over the world and spent her money. My mother used to talk to me all the time about Sicily and I guess I became a typical immigrant child. I knew far more about the place of my birth than I did about my adopted homeland.'

Alannah leaned forward to throw another log on the fire as his words tailed off. 'Go on,' she said.

He watched the flames leap into life. 'When I was old enough, she used to leave me in charge of Michela so she could go travelling with him. She used to sit in casinos, just watching him—though I suspect it was mainly to keep the other women at bay. But he liked the attention—the idea that this rich and wealthy woman had given up everything to be with him. He used to tell her that she was his lucky charm. And I guess for a while that was okay—I mean, the situation certainly wasn't perfect, but it was bearable. Just that beneath the surface everything was crumbling and there was nothing I could do to stop it.'

She heard the sudden darkness in his voice. 'How?'

Leaning his head back against the chair, he half closed his eyes. 'My mother's inheritance was almost gone. The rent on our fancy apartment in Parioli was due and the creditors were circling like vultures. I remember her mounting sense of panic when she confided the bitter truth to me. I was eighteen and working towards going to college, though something told me that was never going to happen. My father found out about a big tournament in Monaco and they drove to France so that he could take part in it.' There was a pause. 'It was supposed to be the solution to all their problems.'

She heard the sudden break in his voice. 'What happened?'

'Oh, he won,' he said. 'In fact, he cleaned up big time. Enough to clear all his debts and guarantee them the kind of future my mother had prayed for.'

'But?' She sensed there was a *but* coming. It hung in the air like a heavy weight about to topple. He lowered his head to look at her and Alannah almost recoiled from the sudden bleakness in his eyes.

'That night they celebrated with too much champagne and decided to set off for Rome, instead of waiting until the morning. They were driving through the Italian alps when they took a bend too fast. They hit the side of the mountain and the car was destroyed.' He didn't speak for a moment and when he did, his words sounded as if they had been carved from stone.

'Neither of them would have known anything about it. At least, that's what the doctors told me.'

'Oh, Niccolò,' she breathed. 'I'm so sorry. Michela told me they'd died in a car crash, but I didn't know the background to the story.'

'Because I kept as much from her as I could. The post-mortem was inconclusive.' His voice hardened. 'Determining the level of alcohol in a…cadaver is always difficult. And no child should have the shame of knowing her father killed her mother because he was on a drunken high after winning at cards.'

She thought how *cold* he sounded—and how ruthless. But that was his default position, wasn't it—and wasn't it somehow understandable in the circumstances? Wasn't much of his behaviour explained by his dreadful legacy? 'You still must have been devastated?' she ventured.

He gave a bitter laugh. 'Do you want the truth? The real and shocking truth? My overriding emotion was one of relief that my father had won so big and that somehow the money got to me intact. It meant that I could pay the rent and clear the debts. It meant that I could send Michela away to school—at thirteen she was getting too much for me to handle. And it meant that I could live my own life. That I could capitalise on his win and make it even bigger. And that's what I did. I bought my first property with that money and by the end of that first year, I had acquired three.'

Alannah nodded. It was funny how when you joined up the dots the bigger picture emerged. Suddenly, she realised why he'd always been so strict with his sister. She saw now that his own controlling nature must have developed as an antidote to his father's recklessness. Financial insecurity had led him to go on and make himself a colossal fortune which nobody could ever bleed away. His wealth was protected, but in protecting it he had set himself in a world apart from other men.

'And did this all happen at Christmas?' she questioned suddenly. 'Is that why you hate the holidays so much?'

'No. That would have been neat, wouldn't it?' He gave a wry smile. 'It's just that Christmas came to symbolise the bleak epicentre of our family life. For me, it was always such an empty festival. My mother would spend vast amounts of money decking out the rooms of our apartment, but she was never there. Even on Christmas Eve she would be sitting like some passive fool on the sidelines while my father played cards. Supposedly bringing him luck, but in reality—checking out that some buxom hostess wasn't coming onto him.'

She winced at the phrase, but suddenly she could understand some of his prejudice towards her, too. For him, buxom women in skimpy clothes were the ones who threatened his parents' relationship. Yet in the end, his puritanical disapproval of her chosen career had done nothing to destroy his powerful lust for her, which must have confused him. And Niccolò didn't do confusion. She'd always known that. Black and white, with nothing in between.

'To me, Christmas always felt as if I'd walked onto a stage set,' he said. 'As if all the props were in place, but nobody knew which lines to say.'

And Alannah realised that she'd done exactly the same. She had tried to create the perfect Christmas.

She'd bought the tree and hung the holly and the mistletoe—but what she had created had been no more real than the empty Christmases of his past.

'Oh, Niccolò—I'm sorry,' she said. 'I had no idea.'

He looked at her and some of the harshness left his face. 'How would you have done? I've never talked about it. Not to anyone.'

'Maybe some time, it might be good to sit down and discuss it with Michela?' she ventured.

'And destroy her memories?'

'False memories are dangerous. And so are secrets. My mother waited until she was dying to tell me that her drink had been spiked and she didn't even know my father's name. I wish she'd shared it with me sooner. I would have liked to have let her know how much I admired her for keeping me.'

His eyes narrowed. 'She sounds an amazing woman.'

'She was.' His words pleased her but she felt vulnerable with his black eyes looking at her in that curiously assessing way. In an effort to distract herself, she got up and went to look out of the window. 'I'm afraid the snow shows no sign of melting?'

'No.'

She turned round. 'I suppose on a practical level we could take down all the decorations if that would make you feel better—and then we could watch that programme on TV which has been generating so much publicity. Have you heard about it? It's called "Stuff Christmas".'

Without warning, he rose from the chair and walked over to her, his shadow enveloping her and suddenly making her feel very small. His ebony gaze flickered over her and she saw that the bitterness in his eyes had been replaced by the much more familiar flicker of desire.

'Or we could do something else, *mia fata*,' he said softly. 'Something much more appealing. Something which I have been aching to do since I walked back in here. I could take you upstairs to bed and make love to you.'

His features were soft with lust and Alannah thought she'd never seen him looking quite so gorgeous. She wanted him just as she always wanted him, but this time her desire was underpinned with something else—something powerful and inexplicable. A need to hold him and comfort him, after everything he'd told her. A need to want to reach out and protect him.

But he'd only told her because of the situation in which they found themselves and she needed to face the truth. He wanted her for sex—*that was all*— and she needed to protect her own vulnerable heart. Maybe it was time to distance herself from him for a while. Give them both a little space.

But by then he was kissing her and it was too late to say anything. Because when he kissed her like that, she was lost.

CHAPTER NINE

Slowly, Niccolò licked at the delicious rosy flesh of Alannah's nipple until eventually she began to stir. Raising her arms above her head, she stretched languorously as the silky tumble of her hair rippled over the pillow like a black banner.

'Niccolò,' she murmured, dark lashes fluttering open to reveal the sleepy denim eyes beneath.

He gave a smile of satisfaction as she somehow turned his name into a breathy little sigh—a variation of the different ways she'd said it throughout the night. She had gasped it. Moaned it. At one point she had even screamed it—her fingernails clawing frantically at his sweat-sheened body as she'd bucked beneath him. He remembered her flopping back onto the pillow afterwards and asking if was it always like this. But he hadn't answered her. He hadn't dared. For once there had been no words in his vocabulary to describe a night which had surpassed any other in his experience. He had come over and over again... in her and on her. And this time he'd remembered to use protection. Hell. Even doing *that* had felt as if it should be included in the pages of the Kama Sutra. He swallowed as he felt the renewed jerk of desire just from thinking about it. No orgasm had ever felt more powerful; no kisses that deep.

He was still trying to work out why. Because he had allowed her to glimpse the bleak landscape of his past—or because he had waited what seemed like a whole lifetime to possess her? He gave another lick. Maybe it was simply that he was discovering she was nothing like the woman he'd thought her to be.

'Niccolò?' she said again.

'Mmm?'

'Is it morning?'

'I think so.' His tongue traced a sinuous path over the creamy flesh and he felt her shiver. 'Though right now I don't really care. Do you?'

'I don't...' He could hear the note of dreamy submission in her voice. 'I don't think so.'

'Good.' He moved his tongue down over her body, feeling himself harden as it trailed a moist path to her belly. But the anatomical significance of that particular spot suddenly began to stab at his conscience and the thought he'd been trying to block now came rushing into his mind. *Was* she pregnant? He felt the painful contraction of his heart until he reminded himself that was a possibility, not a fact—and he only ever dealt with facts. There was nothing he could do about it right now—so why not continue tracking his tongue down over her salty skin and obliterating the nagging darkness of his thoughts with the brief amnesia of pleasure?

He wriggled down the bed and knelt over her, his legs straddling her as he parted her thighs and put his head between them. The dark triangle of hair at their apex was soft and for a moment he just teased at the curly strands with his teeth. She began to writhe as he flickered his tongue with featherlight accuracy against her clitoris, and the fingernails which had begun to claw restlessly at the sheet now moved to grip his shoulders.

She tasted warm and wet against his mouth and her urgent little cries only increased when he captured her circling hips and pinned them firmly against the mattress, so that he could increase the unremitting pressure of his tongue. He could hear her calling his name out. He could feel her spiralling out of control. And suddenly he felt her begin to spasm helplessly against his mouth.

'N-Niccolò!' she breathed. 'Oh, Niccolò.'

His mind and his body were at such a fever-pitch of hunger that he couldn't speak and, urgently, he reached for a condom and eased himself into her slick warmth.

He groaned. She felt so *tight*. Or maybe it was because he felt so big—as if he wanted to explode from the moment he thrust inside her. As if he wanted to come, over and over again. And yet surely she had drained every seed from his body, so that there was nothing left to give?

It seemed she had not. He drove into her until he didn't know where he ended and she began. Until her back began to arch and her eyes to close—each exquisite spasm racking through his body as time seemed to suspend itself, leaving him dazed and breathless.

The silence of the room was broken only by the sound of his own muffled heartbeat.

'I don't know how much more pleasure I can take,' she said eventually and he felt her face pressing against his shoulder.

He turned his head and blew a soft breath onto her cheek. 'Don't you know that you can never have too much pleasure, *mia tentatrice*?'

But Alannah wrinkled her nose as she stared up at the ceiling because she didn't agree. You could. You definitely could. There was always a snake in the garden of Eden—everyone knew that. She thought about all the things he'd confided in her last night. Her heart had softened when she'd heard his story. She'd felt so close to him—and flattered that he had trusted her enough to tell her all that stuff about his past. But that was dangerous, too. If she wasn't careful she could start weaving hopeless fantasies about something which was never intended to last.

She looked over at the window where bright light was shining against the closed curtains. And she realised that it was Christmas morning and last night he'd wanted to leave. She watched as he got out of bed and walked over to the window to pull back the curtains and she blinked as she gazed outside. Thick snow lay everywhere. Branches and bushes were blanketed with the stuff. Against a dove-grey sky the world looked blindingly white and not a sound could be heard and Alannah knew she mustn't let the fairy-tale perfection of the scene in front of her blind her to the reality of their situation.

She put her hands beneath the duvet, her warm belly instinctively recoiling from the icy touch of her fingers.

'We haven't really discussed what's going to happen if I'm pregnant.'

The words hung and shimmered in the air, like the baubles on the unwanted Christmas tree downstairs.

He seemed to choose his words carefully, as if he was walking through a minefield of possibilities.

'Obviously, if such a situation arises—then I will be forced to consider marrying you.'

Alannah did her best not to recoil because he made it sound like someone being forced to drink a bitter draught of poison. She didn't say anything for a moment and when she did, she chose her words as carefully as he had done.

'Before you do, I think there's something you should take into account,' she said quietly. 'Gone are the days when women could be forced to marry against their will—because there's a baby on the way. If I *am* pregnant, then I want my baby to have love—real love. I would want my baby to put contentment before wealth—and satisfaction before ambition. I would want my baby to grow up to be a warm and grounded individual—and, obviously, none of those things would be possible with you as a cynical role model. So don't worry, Niccolò—I won't be dragging you up the aisle any time soon.'

She had expected anger, or a righteous indignation—but she got neither. Instead, his expression remained cool and non-committal. She almost thought she saw a flicker of amusement in those ebony eyes.

'Have you finished?' he said.

She shrugged, wishing she didn't want him so much. 'I guess.'

'Then I'll make coffee.'

He didn't just make coffee. After a bath which

seemed to take for ever to fill, Alannah dressed and went downstairs to find him deftly cracking eggs into a bowl with one hand.

He glanced up. 'Breakfast?'

She grimaced. 'I don't know if I can face eggs.'

'You really should eat something.'

'I suppose so.' She sat down and took the cup of coffee he poured for her and, after a couple of minutes, a plate of scrambled eggs was pushed across the table. She must have been hungrier than she'd thought because she ate it all, before putting her fork down and watching while he finished his own. She thought how he could even make eating look sexy. *Keep your mind fixed on practicalities,* she told herself. 'We ought to investigate the roads,' she said. 'Maybe we can dig ourselves out.'

'Not yet.' His eyes were thoughtful as they surveyed her over the rim of his coffee cup. 'I think we should go for a walk. You look as if you could do with some colour in your cheeks.'

'That's what blusher is supposed to be for.'

He smiled. 'There's a cupboard below the stairs packed with boots and waterproof jackets—why don't we go and investigate?'

They found coats and wrapped up warm and as Niccolò buttoned up her coat Alannah kept reinforcing the same mantra which had been playing in her head all morning. That none of this meant anything. They were just two people who happened to be alone at Christmas, who happened to enjoy having sex with each other.

But the moment they stepped out into the snow, it

was impossible to keep things in perspective. It felt as if nature were conspiring against her. How could she not be affected when it felt as if she'd been transplanted into a magical world, with a man who made her feel so *alive*?

They walked along, their footsteps sinking into the virgin tracks, and she was surprised when he took her hand as they walked along. Funny how something so insignificant could feel so meaningful—especially when she thought about the many greater intimacies they'd shared. Because holding hands could easily masquerade as tenderness and tenderness was shot with its own special kind of danger...

As occasional stray flakes drifted down on their bare heads they talked about their lives. About the reasons he'd come to live in London and her summer holidays in Ireland. She asked how he'd met Alekto Sarantos, and he told her about their mutual friend Murat, the Sultan of Qurhah, and a long-ago skiing trip, when four very alpha men had challenged each other on the slopes.

'I didn't realise you knew Luis Martinez,' she said. 'That *is* Luis Martinez the world-champion racing driver?'

'Ex world champion,' he said, a little testily—and Alannah realised how competitive the four friends must have been.

He told her he hated litter and cars which hogged the middle lane of the motorway and she confided her dislike of drugs and people who ignored shop assistants by talking on their mobile phones. It was as if they had made an unspoken decision to keep the conversation strictly neutral and, unexpectedly, Alannah found herself relaxing. To anyone observing them, they probably looked like an ordinary couple who'd chosen to escape the mad rush of the city to create a dream holiday for themselves. And that was all it was, she reminded herself fiercely. A dream.

'Are you finding this...impossible?' she said. 'Being stuck here with this manufactured Christmas everywhere, when last night you were desperate to leave?'

He kicked at some snow, so that it created a powdery white explosion before falling to the ground. 'No,' he said eventually. 'It's easier than I imagined. You're actually very good company. In fact, I think I enjoy talking to you almost as much as I enjoy kissing you.' His eyes gleamed. 'Although, on second thoughts...'

She turned away, blinking her eyes furiously because kindness was nearly as dangerous as tenderness in helping you to distort reality. But he was getting to her—even though she didn't want him to. Wasn't it funny how a few kind words had the power to make everything seem different? The world suddenly looked bright and vivid, even though it had been bleached of colour. The snow made the berries on the holly bushes stand out like drops of blood and Alannah reached up to bend back a tree branch, watching as it sent a shower of snow arcing through the air, and something bubbled up inside her and made her giggle.

She turned around to find Niccolò watching her, his eyes narrowed against the bright light, and her mouth grew dry as she saw an instantly recognisable hunger in their black depths.

'What…what are we going to do if it doesn't melt?' she said, suddenly breathless.

He leaned forward to touch a gloved finger to her lips. 'Guess,' he said, and his voice was rough.

CHAPTER TEN

HE MADE LOVE to her as soon as they got back—while her cheeks were still cold from the snowy air and her eager fingers icy against his chest as she burrowed beneath his sweater. Alannah lay on the rug in front of the fire, with her arms stretched above her head, wearing nothing but a pair of knickers. And all her shyness and hang-ups seemed like a distant memory as he trailed his lips over every inch of her body.

His fingertips explored her skin with a curiously rapt attention and she found herself reaching for him with a sudden urgency, drawing in a shuddering breath as he eased into her and letting the breath out again like a slow surrender as he lowered his mouth to hers. She loved the contrast of their bodies—his so olive-skinned and dark against her own milky pallor. She liked watching the flicker of flames gilding his flesh and the way his limbs interlocked so perfectly with her own. She loved the way he tipped his head back when he came—and made that low and shuddered moan of delight.

Much later, he pulled his sweater over her head and set about cooking lunch, while she curled up on the sofa and watched him, and suddenly she felt relaxed.

Really and properly relaxed. The cushion behind her back was soft and feathery and her bare toes were warm in the fire's glow.

'It seems *weird*,' she said as he tipped a pile of clean vegetables from the chopping board into a saucepan, 'to see you in the kitchen, looking like you know exactly what you're doing.'

'That's because I do. It isn't exactly rocket science,' he answered drily. 'Unless you think cooking is too complicated for a mere man and that women are naturally superior in the kitchen?'

'Women are naturally superior at many things,' she said airily. 'Though not necessarily at cooking. And you know what I mean. You're a billionaire businessman who runs an international empire. It's strange to see you *scraping carrots*.'

Niccolò gave a soft laugh as he grabbed a handful of fresh herbs, though he recognised that she'd touched a nerve. Just because he *could* cook, didn't mean he did—and it was a long time since he'd done anything like this. Yet wasn't there something uniquely *comforting* about creating a meal from scratch? He'd cooked for his sister in those early days of loss but as she'd got older his responsibilities towards her had lessened. When he had sent her away to school, only the vacations had required his hands-on guardianship. But he had enjoyed his role as quasi-parent and he'd made sure that he carried it out to the best of his ability—the way he tackled everything in his life.

He remembered the trips to the famous Campagna Amica market, near the Circus Maximus. He had taken Michela with him and shown the sulky teenager how to select the freshest vegetables and the finest pieces of fruit. And all the stall-owners had made a fuss of her—slipping her a ripe pear or a small bunch of perfect grapes.

When Michela had finally left home, he had filled every available hour with work—building up his property portfolio with a determination to underpin his life with the kind of security he'd never had. And as his wealth had grown, so had his ability to delegate. These days he always ate out, unless a woman was trying to impress him with her culinary repertoire. His Mayfair fridge was bare, save for coffee and champagne. His apartment was nothing but a base with a bed. It wasn't a home because he didn't *do* home. But as he squeezed lemon juice over the grilled fish he realised how much he had missed the simple routine of the kitchen.

He glanced up to find Alannah still watching him, her bare legs tucked up beneath her. His sweater was much too big for her and it had the effect of making her look unbelievably fragile. Her black hair was spilling down over her shoulders and her blue eyes were shining and something about that almost innocent look of eagerness made his heart contract.

Deliberately, he turned away, reaching for a bottle of prosecco and two glasses. *She's just someone you're trying to get out of your system,* he reminded himself grimly.

His face was composed by the time he handed her a glass. 'Happy Christmas,' he said.

They drank prosecco, lit candles and ate lunch. Afterwards, he made love to her again and they fell asleep on the sofa—and when they awoke, the candles were almost burnt down and outside the starry sky was dark and clear.

Alannah walked over to the window and he wondered if she was aware that her bare bottom was revealed with every step she took.

'I think the snow might be melting,' she said.

He heard the unmistakable note of disappointment in her voice and something inside him hardened. Did she think they could exist in this little bubble for ever, and pretend the rest of the world wasn't out there?

He insisted on loading the dishwasher and making tea to eat with their chocolate. Because any kind of activity was better than sitting there letting his mind keep working overtime.

But action couldn't permanently silence the nagging thoughts which were building inside him and he thought about what she'd said earlier. About putting contentment before wealth and satisfaction before ambition. About not wanting to drag him up the aisle.

Because that was not a decision she alone could make. And if there *was* a baby, then surely there was only one sensible solution, and that solution was marriage.

His jaw tightened. Obviously it was something he'd thought about, in the same way that the young sometimes thought about getting old—as if it would never happen to them. He liked children—and was godfather to several. Deep down, he'd recognised that one day he wanted to be a father and would select a suitable woman to bear his child.

He'd imagined she would be blonde and slightly aloof. Maybe one of those American women who had been brought up on milk and honey and could trace their roots back over generations. The type who kept their emotions on an even keel. The type who didn't believe in fairy tales. The type he felt safe with. It wasn't their trust funds which excited him, but the satisfaction of knowing that they would unknowingly welcome the son of a Corsican bandit into their rarefied drawing rooms.

He stared across the room at Alannah. In no way was she aloof; he had never seen a woman looking quite so accessible. Even with her fingers wrapped chastely around a mug of herb tea, she looked...wild. He felt his throat dry. She touched something deep inside him, something which felt...*dangerous*. Something which took him to the very edges of his self-control. She always had. She spoke to him as nobody else did. She treated him in a way which no one else would dare try.

But the fact remained that she had a background even more unsettled than his own. He had already taken a gamble on her—but surely there was no need to take another. He might not have learnt many lessons at the knee of his father, but one thing he knew was that the more you gambled—the greater your chance of losing. The most sensible thing he could do would be to walk away from her. To keep on walking, without looking back.

He swallowed. Yet if she carried his child—he could walk nowhere. What choice would he have other than to stay with her? To tie himself to someone who no way fitted the image of the kind of woman he wanted to marry. Two mismatched people united by a single incident of careless passion. What future was there in that?

She looked up and her expression grew wary.

'Why are you frowning at me?'

'I didn't realise I was.'

'Actually, frowning isn't really accurate. You were glaring.'

'Was I?' He leaned back in his chair and studied her. 'I've been thinking.'

'Sounds ominous,' she said.

'You do realise that despite all your words of rebellion this morning—I'm going to marry you if you're having my baby?'

Her creamy skin went pink. He saw her fingertips flutter up to touch the base of her neck.

'What...what made you suddenly think of that?'

He saw the flare of hope in her eyes and knew he mustn't feed it, because that wasn't fair. He had a responsibility to tell her the truth and the last thing he wanted was her thinking he was capable of the same emotions as other men. He mustn't fool her into thinking that his icy heart might be about to melt. His mouth hardened. Because that was never going to happen.

'I suddenly realised,' he said slowly, 'that I could never tolerate my son or daughter growing up and calling another man Father.'

'Even though I am the last kind of person you would consider marrying under normal circumstances.'

He met her eyes—but hadn't he always been completely honest with her? Wouldn't she see through a placatory lie to try to make her feel better? 'I guess.'

She put her cup down quickly, as if she was afraid she was going to spill it. 'So this is all about possession?'

'Why wouldn't it be? This child is half mine.'

'*This child* might not even exist!' she choked out. 'Don't you think we ought to wait until we know, before we start having arguments about parental rights?'

'When *can* you find out?'

'I'll do the test when I get back to London,' she said, jumping up from the sofa and dabbing furiously at her eyes with shaking and fisted hands.

The warm and easy atmosphere of earlier had vanished. And how.

Alannah stormed upstairs to splash cold water onto her face and to try to stem the hot tears from springing to her eyes, and yet all she could feel was a growing sense of frustration. She didn't *want* to be like this. She couldn't blame him for what he'd said, just because it didn't fit in with her fantasies. He was only being straight with her. So maybe this was a wake-up call to start protecting herself. To start facing up to facts.

Their fairy-tale Christmas was over.

She went back downstairs and turned on the TV, giving an exaggerated sigh of relief when she heard the weatherman announce that a warm weather front was pushing up from Spain, and the snow was expected to have thawed by late morning.

'Great news,' she said. 'London here we come.'

Niccolò watched as she stomped out of her chair to throw away the untouched mince pies and chocolates and every attempt he made to start a conversation was met with a monosyllabic response. He realised that he'd never been given such cool treatment by a woman before.

But that didn't stop them having sex that night. Very good sex, as it happened. Their angry words momentarily forgotten, he reached for her in the darkness with a passion which she more than matched. In a room washed silver by the full moon, he watched as she arched beneath him and called out his name.

He awoke to the sound of dripping outside the window to find the weatherman's predictions had been accurate and that the snow was melting. Leaving Alannah sleeping, he packed everything up, made a pot of coffee, then went along the lane to find his car.

By the time he drove back to the cottage, she was up and dressed, standing in the middle of the sitting room, clutching a mug—her face pale and her mouth set. He noticed she'd turned the tree lights off and that the room now looked dull and lacklustre.

'Christmas is over,' she said brightly, as if he were a stranger. As if she hadn't been going down on him just a few sweet hours before.

'What about the tree?'

'The woman I hired the cottage from supplied it. She said she'll take it away.'

'Alannah—'

'No,' she said quietly. 'I don't want any protracted stuff, or silly goodbyes. I just want to get back to London and finish up the job you've employed me to do.'

Niccolò felt a flicker of irritation at her suddenly stubborn and uncompromising attitude, but there didn't seem to be a damned thing he could do about it. She was almost completely silent on the journey back as the car slushed its way through the unnaturally quiet streets and, for some reason, the passionate opera he usually favoured while driving now seemed completely inappropriate.

He drove her to Acton and parked up outside her

home, where most of the small nearby houses seemed to be decked with the most garish tinsel imaginable. Someone had even put an inflatable Santa in their cramped front yard.

'Thanks for the lift,' she said, as she reached for the door handle.

'Aren't you going to invite me in?'

She gave him a steady stare. 'Why would I do that?'

'Maybe because we've been sleeping together and I might like to see where you live?'

Alannah hesitated and hated herself for that hesitation. She wondered if secretly she was ashamed of her little home and fearful of how judgemental he might be. Or was it simply an instinctive reaction, because she was unwilling to expose any more of herself to him?

'Okay, come in, then,' she said grudgingly.

'*Grazie,*' came his sardonic reply.

It was shiveringly cold as she unlocked the door. She'd turned the heating down low before the taxi had arrived to take her to the cottage and now the place felt like an ice-box. Niccolò stood in the centre of her small sitting room as she adjusted the thermostat, looking around him like a man who had just found himself in a foreign country and wasn't quite sure what to do. She wondered how he managed to make her furniture look as if it would be better suited to a doll's house.

'Would you like a guided tour?' she said.

'Why not?'

The cramped dimensions meant she needed to be vigilant about tidiness and Alannah was glad there were no discarded pieces of clothing strewn around her bedroom and that the tiny bathroom was neat. But it still felt excruciating as she led him through an apartment in which she'd tried to maximise all available light in order to give an illusion of space. She'd made all the drapes herself from sari material she'd picked up at the local market, and the artwork which hung on the walls was her own. A friend from college had feng-shuied every room, there were pots of herbs lined up on the window sill in the kitchen, and she found the place both restful and creative.

But she wondered how it must seem through Niccolò's eyes, when you could practically fit the entire place into his downstairs cloakroom back in Mayfair.

They walked back into the sitting room and, rather awkwardly, she stood in front of him. He really did seem like a stranger now, she thought—and a terrible sense of sadness washed over her. How weird to think that just a few hours ago he was deep inside her body—making her feel as if she was closer to him than she'd ever been to anyone.

'I would offer you coffee,' she said. 'But I really do want to get on. If Alekto is going to have the apartment ready for his New Year's Eve party, then I need to get cracking.'

'You're planning to work *today*?'

'Of course. What did you think I'd be doing?' she questioned. 'Sobbing into my hankie because our cosy Christmas is over? I enjoyed it, Niccolò. It was an... interesting experience. And you're a great cook as well as a great lover. But you probably know that.'

She made a polite gesture in the direction of the door but he suddenly caught hold of her wrist, and all pretence of civility had gone.

'Haven't you forgotten something?' he iced out, his eyes glittering with unfeigned hostility.

She snatched her hand away, swallowing as she met his gaze. 'No, I haven't. It's not the kind of thing you can easily forget, is it? Don't worry, Niccolò. I'll let you know whether I'm pregnant or not.'

CHAPTER ELEVEN

'I'M NOT PREGNANT.'

Alannah's voice sounded distorted—as if it were coming from a long way away, instead of just the other side of his desk—and Niccolò didn't say anything—at least, not straight away. He wondered why his heart had contracted with something which felt like pain. Whether he'd imagined the cold taste of disappointment which was making his mouth bitter. He must have done. Because wasn't this the news he'd been longing for? The only sane solution to a problem which should never have arisen?

He focused his eyes to where Alannah sat perched on the edge of a chair opposite him and thought how pale she looked. Paler than the thick white lanes through which they'd walked on Christmas Day, when the snow had trapped them in that false little bubble. Her blue eyes were ringed with dark shadows, as if she hadn't been sleeping.

Had she?

Or had she—like he—been lying wide-eyed in the depths of the night, remembering what it had felt like when they'd made love and then fallen asleep with their limbs tangled warmly together?

He flattened the palms of his hands flat on the surface of his desk. 'You're sure?'

'One hundred per cent.'

He wondered why she had chosen to tell him here, and now. Why she had come to his office after successfully negotiating a ten-minute slot in his diary with Kirsty. And Kirsty hadn't even checked with him first!

'Couldn't you have chosen a more suitable time and place to tell me, rather than bursting into my office and getting my assistant to collude with you?' he questioned impatiently. 'Or is it just a continuation of your determination to keep me at arm's length?'

'I've been busy.'

That was usually *his* excuse. He leaned back in his chair and studied her. 'You won't even have dinner with me,' he observed coolly.

'I'm sure you'll get over it,' she said lightly.

His gaze didn't waver. 'I thought you said you'd enjoyed our "experiment" over Christmas—so why not run with it a little longer? Come on, Alannah.' A smile curved his lips. 'What harm could it do?'

Alannah stared at him. What *harm* could it do? Was he serious? But that was the trouble—he was. Unemotional, cynical and governed by nothing but sexual hunger—Niccolò obviously saw no reason why they shouldn't continue with the affair. Because it meant different things to each of them. For him, it was clearly just an enjoyable diversion, while for her it felt as if someone had chipped away a little bit of her heart every time she saw him. *It was being chipped away right now.*

She had chosen his office and a deliberately short

appointment in which to tell him her news in order to avoid just this kind of scene. She'd actually considered telling him by phone but had instinctively felt that such a move would have been counterproductive. That he might have insisted on coming round to confront her face to face and her defences would have been down.

It was bad enough trying to stay neutral now—even with the safety of his big oak desk between them. Sitting there in his crisp white shirt and tailored suit, Niccolò's face was glowing with health and vitality and she just wanted to go and put her arms around him. She wanted to lean on him and have him tell her that everything was going to be okay. But he didn't want a woman like her leaning on him and anyway—she was independent and strong. She didn't need a man who could never give her what she wanted, and what she wanted from him was love. *Join the queue,* she thought bitterly.

'You haven't *done* anything,' she said. 'You haven't made or broken any promises. Everything is how it's supposed to be, Niccolò. What happened between us was great but it was never intended to last. And it hasn't.'

'But what if…?' He picked up the golden pen which was lying on top of the letters he'd been signing and stared at it as if he had never really seen it before. He lifted his gaze to hers. 'What if I wanted it to last—at least for a little while longer? What then?'

Alannah tensed as fear and yearning washed over her—yet of the two emotions, the yearning was by far the deadlier.

'And how long did you have in mind?' she questioned sweetly. 'One week? Two? Would it be presumptuous to expect it might even continue for a *whole month*?'

He slammed the pen down. 'Does it matter?' he demanded. 'Not every relationship between a man and a woman lasts for ever.'

'But most relationships don't start out with a discussion about when it's going to end!' She sucked in a breath and prayed she could hold onto her equilibrium for a while longer. 'Look, nothing has changed. I'm still the same woman I always was—except that I have you to thank for helping me lose some of my inhibitions. But I still don't know who my father was and I still have the kind of CV which would make someone with your sensitive social antennae recoil in horror. Appearances matter to you, Niccolò. You know they do. So why don't you just celebrate the fact that you had a lucky escape and that we aren't going to be forced together by some random act of nature.' She rose to her feet. 'And leave me to finish off Alekto's apartment in time for his party. The caterers are arriving tomorrow, and there are still some last-minute touches which need fixing.'

'Sit down,' he said. 'I haven't finished yet.'

'Well, I have. We've said everything which needs to be said. It's over, Niccolò. I'm not so stupid that I want to hang around having sex with a man who despises everything I stand for!'

'I don't despise what you stand for. I made a lot of judgements about you and some of them were wrong.'

'Only *some* of them?' she demanded.

'Why can't you just accept what I'm offering? Why do you have to want more?'

'Because I'm worth it.' She hitched the strap of her handbag over her shoulder. 'And I'm going now.'

He rose to his feet. 'I don't want you to go!' he gritted out.

'Tough. I'm out of here. *Ciao.*'

And to Niccolò's amazement she picked up her handbag and walked out of his office without a backward glance.

For a moment he stood there, stunned—as the door slammed behind her. He thought about rushing after her, about pulling her into his arms and kissing her and *then* seeing whether she was so damned certain their relationship was over. But that would make it all about sex, wouldn't it? And sex had always been the least troublesome part of this equation. Besides, Kirsty was buzzing through to tell him that his eleven o'clock had arrived, so he was forced to concentrate on listening to what his architect was saying, rather than on a pair of stubborn pink lips he still wanted to crush beneath his own.

By seven o'clock that evening, he decided that Alannah had been right. Better to end it now, before she got in too deep—because it wouldn't be fair to break her heart as he had broken so many others. She would start falling in love with him. She would want more from him than he was capable of giving. Better they both recognised his limitations now.

He glanced up at the clock again. Maybe he should start as he meant to go on. Dinner with someone new would surely be the way to go. A civilised dinner with someone who didn't get under his skin the way she did.

He flicked through his address book, but none of the long list of names excited him enough to pick up the phone. He had his driver drop him home and worked in his study until way past midnight. But still he couldn't sleep. He kept remembering when Alannah had spent the night with him there and, even though the linen had been laundered, he thought he could still detect the unique scent of her skin on his sheets. He thought about the cottage. About the tree-lights and the snow. About that unreal sense of quiet satisfaction as he had cooked her Christmas lunch. The way they had fallen asleep on the sofa after they'd made love. Hadn't that been like the closest thing to peace he'd felt in a long, long time?

And that was all make-believe, he told himself fiercely. As insubstantial as Christmas itself.

He lay and watched the luminous numbers on his clock changing slowly and just before his alarm was due to go off a text arrived from Alekto Sarantos.

Don't be late for my party! Beautiful women and a beautiful apartment—what better way to see in the new year? A

Niccolò stared blankly at the screen of his mobile phone, telling himself that a party was exactly what he needed, and didn't Alekto throw some of the best parties he'd ever been to? But just the thought of it left him cold. Tugging on his running gear, he got ready for the gym and wondered why his eyes looked so shadowed and haunted.

But deep down, he knew exactly why.

'It is *spectacular.*' Alekto Sarantos smiled as he looked around the main reception room, his blue eyes gleaming. 'You have transformed my apartment, Al-annah—and you have worked against the clock to get it done in time for my party. *Efkaristo poli.* I thank you.'

Alannah smiled back, even though just smiling seemed to take a massive effort these days. It was true that the place *did* look pretty amazing—especially when she thought back to the sea of beige it had been before. The woman who had made the curtains had got very excited about it and she had told someone, who had told someone else. Even during the short period between Christmas and new year, word had soon got round in an industry which survived by constantly seeking out new ideas and new faces. Already Alannah had received a phone call from one of the big interior magazines, asking if they could do a photo shoot there. She doubted whether Alekto would agree, since she got the idea he was very hot on privacy. Still, she could *always ask* him. And even if he didn't give his permission, she sensed that she had turned a corner—because this was the big break she had been waiting for. *And she had Niccolò to thank for it.*

Security and creative fulfilment were lying within her grasp. So why did it all feel so empty? Why was she having to force herself to look and sound enthusiastic about something she'd always dreamed of?

She sighed. She knew *exactly* why. *Because she'd made the fundamental mistake of falling in love with a man who had never offered her anything but sex.*

'I hope you're coming to my new year's party?' Alekto was saying. 'You really ought to be the guest of honour, after what you've achieved here. Unless, of course, you have already made plans?'

Alannah glanced out at the late afternoon sky, which was now almost dark. The only plans she had made were to buy the TV guide and turn up the central heating, while she waited for Big Ben to chime in a new year she couldn't seem to get worked up about. She thought about getting dressed up for a party attended by Alekto Sarantos and his glamorous friends, and how any sane person would leap at such an opportunity.

But what if Niccolò was there?

Her heart pounded. The possibility was high. It was more than high. They were best mates, weren't they? She shook her head. 'It's very sweet of you— but I think I'll just have a quiet evening in,' she said.

'Up to you.' Alekto shrugged. 'But if you change your mind...'

Alannah went home, bathed and washed her hair— before pulling on her dressing gown and a pair of slouchy socks and switching on the TV. She flicked channels. Crowds of people were already flocking into Trafalgar Square, even though it was still early. People were being interviewed, swigging from beer bottles and giggling—and Alannah suddenly saw herself as a fly on the wall might see her. A woman sitting on her own at nine o'clock on New Year's Eve, wearing a dressing gown and a pair of old socks.

What had she become?

She swallowed. She had become a cliché, that was what. She had fallen in love with someone who had always been out of reach. And yet, instead of accepting that and holding her head up high and just getting on with her life, the way she'd always done, she had caved in. She was like some sort of mole, living in darkness—cowering inside her own safe little habitat, because she was afraid to go out. It was the worst night of the year to be home alone—especially if your stupid heart was heavy and aching—and yet here she was. *Mole.*

What was she so worried about? That she might see Niccolò with another woman? Surely that would be the best of all possible outcomes—it would remind her of how easily he could move on. It would make her accept *reality*, instead of chasing after rainbows.

Tearing off her slouchy socks, she pulled out the gold dress she'd worn at Christmas and slithered into it. Then she slapped on a defiant amount of make-up, her highest heels—and a warm, ankle-length coat. People were milling outside pubs as she made her way to the station and more snow was falling as she caught the underground and got out at Knightsbridge.

It was much quieter in this part of town. There were few revellers out and about around here—this was the world of the private, rather than the street party. But by the time she reached Park View other partygoers were milling around in the foyer and the party atmosphere was contagious. She shared the elevator up to Alekto's apartment with several stunning women and a man who kept surreptitiously glancing at his phone.

The elevator pinged to a halt and the door to the penthouse was opened by a waitress dressed as a flamingo, a tray of exotic-looking cocktails in her hand. Alannah went off to hang up her coat and then wandered along the corridors she knew so well, back towards the sitting room. It was strange seeing the place like this—full of people—when she had only ever seen it empty. Most of the furniture she'd installed had been pushed back against the walls to maximise the space—but the room still looked spectacular. Even she could see that. The colours worked brilliantly—providing the perfect backdrop for Alekto's extensive art collection—and she was particularly proud of the lighting.

In spite of everything, she knew Niccolò would be pleased with her work. He might regret some things, but he would never regret giving her the job and she should take pride in that. A horrible dark pain washed over her, only this time it was underpinned with reproach. She wasn't supposed to be thinking about Niccolò. Wasn't that going to be her one and only new year resolution? That part of her life was over. She had to cut her losses and move on. And it was a waste of time to wonder what it would have been like if she *had* been pregnant. Or to dwell on that irrational and sinking sense of disappointment when she had stared at the test result and it had been negative.

A woman masquerading as a bird of paradise offered her a drink and Alannah took one, but the sweet concoction tasted deceptively powerful and she put the glass down as Alekto Sarantos came over to talk to her.

'You made it, then,' he said, with a smile. '*Thavmassios.* If I had a Euro for every person who has asked me who is responsible for the design of this apartment, then I would be a very rich man.'

'But I thought you *were* a very rich man,' she said, and he laughed, before giving her a thoughtful look. 'I might have some work for you in Greece, if you're interested?'

Alannah didn't even need to think about it. 'I'd be very interested,' she said immediately, because a different country might be just what she needed. What was it they said? A new year and a new start.

'Why don't you call my office on Monday?' he suggested, pulling out a business card and handing it to her.

'I will,' she said, putting it into her handbag as he walked away.

'Alannah?'

A familiar voice curled over her skin like dark velvet and she turned to see Niccolò standing there. His hair and shoulders were wet with melting snow and he was wearing a dark cashmere coat, which made him stand out from all the other guests. Alannah stiffened as his shadow fell over her and her heart began to hammer as she looked up into his shuttered features.

The knot of tension in her stomach grew tighter. But she had come here tonight to hold her head high, hadn't she? Not to hang it in shame. Nor to waste time wishing for something which could never be.

'Niccolò,' she said coolly. 'Fancy seeing you here.'

'What were you saying to Alekto?'

'That's really none of your business.'

'You do know he is world-famous for breaking women's hearts?'

'Why, has he lifted the crown from you?' she questioned acidly. 'And what are you doing still wearing your overcoat?'

'Because I have driven halfway across London looking for you,' he growled.

She frowned. 'Why?'

'Why do you think?' he exploded. 'I went round to your apartment, only you weren't there.' He had spent the afternoon psyching himself up, making careful plans about what he was going to say to her. He had decided to surprise her, because he...well, because he wanted to—and that in itself was uncharacteristic. He had naturally made the assumption that she would have been home alone, only when he'd got there Alannah's apartment had been shrouded in darkness and his heart had sunk. The sight of all those empty windows had suddenly seemed like a metaphor for his life and they had confirmed the certainty which had been growing inside him for days.

Instinct had made him pull out his telephone to speak to Alekto and his hunch was proved right. His friend had coolly informed him that, yes, Alannah *had* been invited to the party and although she'd told him she wasn't coming, she seemed to have changed her mind. In fact, she had just walked in, looking like a goddess in a spectacular golden dress.

Niccolò had turned his car around and driven from Acton, getting snarled up in the new-year traffic—his nerves becoming more and more frayed as an unfamiliar sense of agitation nagged away at him. And now he was here standing in front of her and nothing was as he thought it would be. He had not intended to launch into a jealous tirade because he'd seen her being chatted up by one of the world's biggest players.

Wasn't he supposed to be a 'player' himself?

His mouth hardened.

Not any more.

He was in a roomful of some of the most beautiful

women in the world and yet he could see only one. One who was staring at him with hostility and suspicion and, in his heart, he knew he couldn't blame her.

So why the hell was he demonstrating an arrogance which might cause her magnificent pride to assert itself, and tell him to take a running jump? He needed to keep her onside. To placate her. To make her realise why he had come here. *And to make her realise that it was the only possible solution.*

'I need to talk to you,' he said.

'Talk away.' She gave a careless shrug. 'I'm not stopping you.'

'In private.'

'I'd prefer to stay here, if you don't mind.'

'Unfortunately, *tentatrice*, I do mind.'

Without warning, he caught hold of her hand, his fingers enclosing her hammering pulse as he led her through the throng of partygoers until they had reached one of the bedrooms. He shut the door, just as she shook her hand free and glared at him.

'What do you think you're doing?' she demanded. 'You can't just waltz up to someone in the middle of a party and *manhandle* them like that! You can't just drag a woman from a room because you've decided you want a private word with her. Oh, sorry—I'd forgotten.' She slapped her palm against her brow. 'You can—and you do. Well, you might be Tarzan but I am not your Jane. I don't *do* Neanderthal and I don't *do* arrogant men who think they can just blaze into other people's lives doing exactly what they want. So will you please step aside and let me pass?'

'Not until you've heard me out,' he said, as a strange sense of calm washed over him. 'Please.'

She looked at him for a moment before pointedly glancing at her watch. 'You've got five minutes.'

Niccolò sucked in a breath but for a moment he couldn't speak. His calmness seemed to be deserting him as he realised that this wasn't going to be easy. He was going to have to do something unheard of—something he had instinctively always shied away from. He was going to have to pull out his feelings from the dark place where he'd buried them and he was going to have to admit them. To her. And even when he did, there was no guarantee that it might not be too late.

He looked into the wary blue of her eyes and his heart pounded. 'I need to ask your forgiveness,' he said. 'For all the unjust accusations I hurled at you. For my bull-headedness and my lack of compassion. For taking so long to realise the kind of woman you really are. Strong and proud and passionate and loyal. I've missed you, Alannah, and I want you back. Nobody talks to me the way you do, or makes me feel the way you do. Nobody else makes my heart skip a beat whenever I see her. I want to spend the rest of my life with you. To one day make the baby we didn't have this time. I want to make a real home—with you. Only with you.'

She took a step back, as if she'd just seen a ghost, and she started shaking her head. 'You don't want me,' she said in a hoarse voice. 'You only think you do, because I'm the one who walked away and that's probably never happened to you before. You want someone respectable, who is as pure as the driven snow—because that's the sort of thing you care about. Someone *suitable*. You didn't want me as bridesmaid because you were worried about what other people would think. Because you're hung up on appearances and how things look from the outside, no matter what you say.'

'I used to be,' he said savagely. 'But you have made me realise that appearances and social position don't matter. It's what's underneath which counts. And you have everything that counts. You are soft and smart and funny. You are kind and caring and talented. You didn't even smoke dope at school, did you— even though you were accused of it?'

Startled by this sudden conversational twist, Alannah narrowed her eyes suspiciously. 'Did Michela tell you that?'

He shook his head. 'She didn't have to. I worked it out for myself. I think you may just have covered up for my sister all this time.'

'Because that's what friends do,' she said fiercely. 'That's called loyalty.'

'I realise that now,' he said. 'It's just taken me a long and very circuitous route to get here. But I don't want to talk about the past any more... I want to concentrate on the future.'

He reached within the pocket of his snow-covered overcoat and pulled out a little box. 'This is for you,' he said, and his voice was slightly unsteady.

Alannah watched as he opened it and she was shamefully aware of a sinking sense of disappointment as she looked inside. Had she really thought it was an engagement ring? Was she really that fickle? Because glittering against the background of dark velvet was a brooch shaped like a little honey-bee. Its back was covered with yellow, black and white stones and she found herself thinking that she'd never seen anything so sparkly. She looked up at him, still disorientated.

'What's this?' she said.

'You collect insect brooches, don't you? They're diamonds. The black ones are quite rare. It's for you,' he said again. 'Because I didn't buy you a Christmas present.'

But Alannah felt a terrible lump in her throat as she began to blink her eyes rapidly. 'You just don't get it, do you?' she whispered. 'The brooches I have are all worth peanuts. I wear them because my mother gave them to me—because they *mean* something to me. I don't care if they're diamonds or paste, Niccolò. I don't care how much something is *worth.*'

'Then what if I tell you this is worth what I feel for you, and that is everything. *Everything.*' He moved closer. 'Unless you want me to go to a flea-market to find you something cheaper? Tell me, Alannah—are you going to set me a series of challenges before you will accept me?'

She almost laughed, except that now hot tears were springing to her eyes and she couldn't seem to stop them. 'I don't know what I'm going to do,' she whispered. 'Because I'm scared. Scared because I keep thinking this is all a dream and that I'm going to wake up in a minute.'

'No, not a dream,' he said, taking the brooch from the box and pinning it next to the little grasshopper which already adorned her golden dress. 'I bought you this because I love you. This is the reality.'

Her lips parted. 'Niccolò,' she said again, and now her voice was shaking. 'If this isn't true—'

He halted her protest by placing his finger over her lips. 'It *is* true. It has always been true. The first time I set eyes on you, I was hit by a thunderbolt so powerful that I felt as if you'd cast some kind of spell on me. And that spell never really faded. I love you, Alannah—even though I've been running away from the idea of love all my life. I saw what it did to my mother. I saw it as a weakness which sucked the life from everything in its path. Which blinded her even to the needs of her children.'

She bit her lip. 'I can understand that.'

He sensed her absolution, but he was not finished. 'But what I feel for you does not feel like weakness. I feel strong when I am with you, Alannah. As strong as a mountain lion. As if I could conquer the world.'

She let him put his arms around her and her head rested against his chest. 'That's funny, because right now I feel as weak as a kitten.'

His black eyes burned into her as he gently levered her face up so that she was looking directly at him. 'The only thing I need to know is whether you love me?'

'Of course I love you.' The words came tumbling out as if she'd been waiting all her life to say them. She thought about the first time she'd seen him, when they'd just clicked. It had been a thunderbolt for her, too, and she had never been able to forget him. She thought about how empty her life seemed when he wasn't there. He wasn't the man she'd thought him to be—he was so much more. 'I think I've always loved you.'

'Then kiss me, my beautiful Alannah,' he said softly. 'And let me show you my love.'

Slowly and tenderly, he traced his fingertip along the edges of her lips before lowering his head towards hers and Alannah's heart filled up with so much happiness that she felt as if she might burst with it.

EPILOGUE

'I USED TO think you hated weddings.'

Niccolò looked down into Alannah's face as he closed the door to their honeymoon suite, and smiled at her. 'I did. But that was before I found the woman I wanted to marry. Now it seems that I'm their biggest fan.'

'Mmm. Me, too.' She looped her arms around his neck. 'You did like the dress?'

'You looked beautiful. The most beautiful bride in the world. But then, you could wear a piece of sacking and I still wouldn't be able to tear my eyes away from you.'

'Oh, Niccolò.' She slanted him a look from between her lashes. 'Whoever would have guessed that beneath that cynical exterior beat the heart of a true poet?'

'It's true,' he said, mock-seriously. 'Though I must be careful not to lose my edge. If my competitors find out how much I'm softening, then I will soon be toast in the world of finance.'

'You?' She laughed easily. 'Yeah, sure. Like *that's* ever going to happen!'

He began to unzip her dress. 'Are you tired?'

'Not a bit. Even though it's been a very long day.'

She closed her eyes as the costly gown pooled to the ground around her feet. She had thought he would want a quiet wedding—something discreet, even a little hushed-up. Hadn't she thought he'd want to keep the risk of press interest to a minimum, despite his protestations that her past no longer bothered him? Probably. But once again he had surprised her. It was funny how love had the power to change people and to alter their views on what was important. He had told her that he was going to announce their engagement to the world's press and then he had gone out and bought her an enormous sapphire ring, which he said was the closest colour he could get to the denim-blue of her eyes.

Predictably, some of the old photos from *Stacked* magazine had made an appearance in the papers—but suddenly, they didn't seem to matter. It was slightly surreal to hear Niccolò echoing his sister's words—*and believing them*—by saying really they were very tame in comparison to a lot of the stuff you saw in contemporary music videos.

'I am proud of you, *tentatrice*,' he had murmured, crumpling the newspaper into a ball and hurling it into the bin. 'Proud of all you have achieved and how you have kept your dignity intact. Most of all, I am proud that you have consented to be my wife.'

And she had smiled. 'Oh, darling.'

The wedding was held in London's oldest Italian church, in Clerkenwell, and there was a stellar number of guests. A fully recovered Luis Martinez was there—as was the Sultan of Qurhah, Murat 'the Magnificent'. And naturally, Alekto Sarantos was at his dazzling best, even though he was barely visible through the sea of eager women who were clamouring round him. Michela was matron of honour—her silk gown cleverly hiding the beginning of a baby bump.

With Alannah's encouragement, Niccolò had told Michela the truth about their parents' death—and the admission had brought brother and sister much closer. Because secrets were always more dangerous than the truth, as he'd learned.

Alannah shivered with pleasure as Niccolò lifted her out of the discarded wedding dress and carried her over to the bed, wearing nothing but her underwear, sheer stockings and a pair of very high, white stilettos. As he undressed her she thought about the inhibitions which had once crippled her and which now seemed like a distant memory.

Tomorrow they were flying to the island of Niccolò's birth. He had only been back to Sicily once, after his mother's death—when he had been full of youthful rage and bitterness about the rejection she had suffered at the hands of her own family. But time had mellowed him and Alannah had helped him get some perspective. His maternal grandparents were dead—but he had cousins and uncles and aunts living there. A whole new family for them to get to know. And she was excited about that, too—looking forward to a big, extended family after so many years on her own.

He moved over her, his face suddenly very serious as he brushed her hair away from her cheek. 'Thank you,' he said softly.

She took his hand and kissed it. 'For?'

'For loving me. For being you.'

For being you. He didn't want anyone else, she had come to realise. He just wanted her exactly as she was, with no changes or modifications. He didn't want to rewrite her past, or pretend it hadn't happened, because her past had made her the woman she was today. And he loved that woman.

Alannah sighed.

Just like she loved her man.

* * * * *

Mills & Boon® Hardback
December 2014

ROMANCE

MEDICAL

Mills & Boon® Large Print
December 2014

ROMANCE

Zarif's Convenient Queen	Lynne Graham
Uncovering Her Nine Month Secret	Jennie Lucas
His Forbidden Diamond	Susan Stephens
Undone by the Sultan's Touch	Caitlin Crews
The Argentinian's Demand	Cathy Williams
Taming the Notorious Sicilian	Michelle Smart
The Ultimate Seduction	Dani Collins
The Rebel and the Heiress	Michelle Douglas
Not Just a Convenient Marriage	Lucy Gordon
A Groom Worth Waiting For	Sophie Pembroke
Crown Prince, Pregnant Bride	Kate Hardy

HISTORICAL

Beguiled by Her Betrayer	Louise Allen
The Rake's Ruined Lady	Mary Brendan
The Viscount's Frozen Heart	Elizabeth Beacon
Mary and the Marquis	Janice Preston
Templar Knight, Forbidden Bride	Lynna Banning

MEDICAL

200 Harley Street: The Soldier Prince	Kate Hardy
200 Harley Street: The Enigmatic Surgeon	Annie Claydon
A Father for Her Baby	Sue MacKay
The Midwife's Son	Sue MacKay
Back in Her Husband's Arms	Susanne Hampton
Wedding at Sunday Creek	Leah Martyn

Mills & Boon® Hardback
January 2015

ROMANCE

MEDICAL

Mills & Boon® Large Print
January 2015

ROMANCE

The Housekeeper's Awakening	Sharon Kendrick
More Precious than a Crown	Carol Marinelli
Captured by the Sheikh	Kate Hewitt
A Night in the Prince's Bed	Chantelle Shaw
Damaso Claims His Heir	Annie West
Changing Constantinou's Game	Jennifer Hayward
The Ultimate Revenge	Victoria Parker
Interview with a Tycoon	Cara Colter
Her Boss by Arrangement	Teresa Carpenter
In Her Rival's Arms	Alison Roberts
Frozen Heart, Melting Kiss	Ellie Darkins

HISTORICAL

Lord Havelock's List	Annie Burrows
The Gentleman Rogue	Margaret McPhee
Never Trust a Rebel	Sarah Mallory
Saved by the Viking Warrior	Michelle Styles
The Pirate Hunter	Laura Martin

MEDICAL

200 Harley Street: The Shameless Maverick	Louisa George
200 Harley Street: The Tortured Hero	Amy Andrews
A Home for the Hot-Shot Doc	Dianne Drake
A Doctor's Confession	Dianne Drake
The Accidental Daddy	Meredith Webber
Pregnant with the Soldier's Son	Amy Ruttan

MILLS & BOON®

Why shop at millsandboon.co.uk?

Each year, thousands of romance readers find their perfect read at millsandboon.co.uk. That's because we're passionate about bringing you the very best romantic fiction. Here are some of the advantages of shopping at www.millsandboon.co.uk:

* **Get new books first**—you'll be able to buy your favourite books one month before they hit the shops

* **Get exclusive discounts**—you'll also be able to buy our specially created monthly collections, with up to 50% off the RRP

* **Find your favourite authors**—latest news, interviews and new releases for all your favourite authors and series on our website, plus ideas for what to try next

* **Join in**—once you've bought your favourite books, don't forget to register with us to rate, review and join in the discussions

Visit **www.millsandboon.co.uk**
for all this and more today!